THE NAUGHTY ONE

A DOCTOR'S CHRISTMAS ROMANCE (SEASON OF DESIRE 2)

MICHELLE LOVE

HOT AND STEAMY ROMANCE

CONTENTS

Made in "The United States" by:

Michelle Love

© Copyright 2021

ISBN: 978-1-64808-826-1

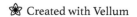 Created with Vellum

BLURB

Romy Sasse, a young surgical resident, returns to her hometown Seattle and immediately meets her new boss, superstar surgeon, Blue Allende. The attraction between them is immediate and intense, and there's a twist ...

Romy's mom is about to marry Blue's father.
Soon, Blue and Romy are falling in love, and enjoying a steamy, sizzling relationship. Finally, Romy feels she has escaped her past and her violent ex.
As Christmas approaches, however, a series of horrific murders brings the past back to haunt the couple and they face the most serious test to their love yet ...
Will the Holiday Season bring resolution and a Happy Ever After?

Doctors in love?
Romy Sasse doesn't want to fall for her surgical superstar boss Blue Allende,
But the gorgeous doctor makes it clear: he wants her.
Soon, they cannot deny their attraction, and begin a steamy affair ...

With Christmas coming, and the marriage of Blue's father and
Romy's mother,
Romy and Blue soon become inseparable. But when dark secrets and
lies threaten their love, neither can tell if their love will survive ...

Young surgical resident Romy Sasse returns home to Washington
State for the holidays to find her free-spirited mother has become
engaged to the last person Romy would expect—multi-billionaire,
Stuart Eames. As both of the families gather for Thanksgiving, Romy
meets Stuart's son, financier Gaius, and immediately takes a dislike to
him. Her world is turned upside down, however, when she discovers
Stuart's other illegitimate son is none other than her new boss,
surgical god, Blue Allende.
Inspired by Blue's expertise in the operating theater, Romy is grateful
when he decides to mentor her though her last year as a surgical
resident, and soon it becomes clear that their chemistry extends
further than the hospital. At first, Romy resists temptation; she
doesn't want to be seen as the doctor who slept her way to the top.
But soon, the attraction between them becomes undeniable.
Marring her happiness, Romy finds that divisions with Blue's family
go deep. Gaius is psychotically jealous of his younger, illegitimate
half-brother and will stop at nothing to ruin his career and his life.
Having already made unreciprocated advances towards Romy, Gaius
is outraged when Blue and Romy fall in love. As Christmas
approaches and a severe ice storm hits Seattle, Gaius, with the help of
anther malevolent force from Romy's past, unleashes a campaign of
terror which will not only test their skills in the operating theater, but
risk their lives and

their love as well ...

1
CHAPTER 1

*S*eattle

ROMY SHOVED her chestnut brown hair up into a ponytail as she jogged quickly along the hospital corridors. *Damn Seattle traffic.* She had been so organized right up until she'd hit the traffic accident on the Alaskan Way viaduct. Now she'd missed the first few minutes of rounds, and on the worst possible day. So not a good first impression to make. Still cursing herself, she hurried to catch up with her colleagues in the general surgery department.

Rounding the corner at a fast clip, she heard his voice before she saw him, a deep, mellifluous tone which she knew made woman weak. She might never have met the man, but his voice was as legendary as his surgical skills. Oh yeah. And his body. People talked about that in the same breath as his medical accomplishments.

He spoke again and she thrilled at the husky hint of an accent— Italian, maybe?—in it.

"If the infection worsens we'll consider a shunt, but in all likelihood, it will resolve rapidly since it was caught at the outset."

Romy blinked in surprise at the words. Blue Allende, he of the oh-so-sexy voice, was a superstar surgeon. Not even forty years old, he was at the top of his game, and also at the top of most hospital's wish-lists. With the reputed looks of a movie star and the serious, brooding intelligence of someone a lot older, Blue Allende's reputation preceded him. So why was he standing around with a motley crew of doctors, nurses, and interns, discussing something as mundane as a shunt?

It gave her pause and jumpstarted her liking for the man who, apparently, wasn't your average arrogant genius surgeon. But Romy was still late, and no doctor appreciated tardiness, particularly not one with such a packed schedule ...

Goddamn it.

Stopping outside the door she saw a bunch of other residents and slipped in among them, hoping she wouldn't be noticed and knowing she didn't stand a prayer.

Her friend Mac, an affable African American with a sweet face and a wicked sense of humor, grinned and nudged her. "Late for the rockstar, Sasse," he hissed, "*genius* move."

Romy poked him with her elbow, rolling her eyes. "What did I miss?"

Suddenly the crowd of doctors parted and she saw him where he'd been leaning over a sedated patient. Her breath caught in her throat as Blue Allende turned bright green eyes on her.

All the usual hospital noises faded into the background as she was caught in that fiercely intelligent gaze.

Jesus, Romy thought, *this man doesn't belong in an operating theater; he belongs on a cat walk or on the cover of* Vogue.

He was *gorgeous*. The bright green eyes were surrounded by thick, black eyelashes on a face carved from Italian marble. A shock of dark curls fell messily about his head ... then she noticed his wide, sensual mouth set in a thin line.

Ah, shit. She'd like to have seen that mouth in something other than a scowl.

"Dr. Sasse, welcome."

That voice from up close. *Wowwowwow.* And ... he knew her name? Romy prayed not to stutter. "Apologies for my tardiness, Dr. Allende; it won't happen again."

Was that a hint of amusement that flashed in those devastatingly beautiful eyes, and maybe a slight hitching up of the mouth? No sooner had Romy thought she'd seen it than it was gone. He turned back to his patient and Romy was grateful he hadn't shamed her in front of everyone else. One more point in his favor, bigtime.

"Got away with it," Mac muttered in her ear, and Romy sighed with relief.

As they moved through rounds, she was impressed by Allende's in-depth knowledge of his cases and the way he coaxed the residents to find answers to his questions, rather than merely lecturing. Even when they got a fact wrong, he didn't sneer or bark at them. Furthermore, he treated patients like friends, addressing them with as much candor as compassion, taking his time rather than rushing right along.

More than slightly blown away by the whole picture, Romy watched him carefully and was confused when she spotted him in an unguarded moment when the group was discussing a situation and he apparently thought no one was paying attention to him. Also not typical. Grandstanding surgeons believed the spotlight was always on them. In that brief second though, she saw something in his eyes that she recognized all too well.

Pain. Sorrow.

Romy was so distracted by the revelation that she didn't realize the focus had shifted and everyone was staring at her. Suddenly feeling the heat of their stares, she swallowed hard, flushing. "I'm sorry, Dr. Allende, could you repeat the question?"

The amused look was back, displacing sorrow. "I was asking if you could give me the ways we can use to diagnose *ankylosing spondylitis*?"

Romy cleared her throat. "Of course." She ran through the

options and then concluded, "Of course, the disease is notoriously hard to diagnose, and once identified, it usually is a case of pain management. Opioids have little effect pain-wise, but we could try medical marijuana as a last resort."

"Hail Mary," said the patient, a young man in his twenties, and they all laughed.

"As a *last* resort, Billy." Blue smiled and Romy's entire body reacted to it. It lit up his handsome face and Romy could feel a beat pulsing between her legs. *Stop it,* she told herself, *do not get a crush on your boss.*

AFTER ROUNDS, Blue asked to see her in his office. He motioned to the chair opposite his desk and Romy sat down, trembling with nervousness. Was she about to be bawled out for being late?

"Don't look so scared," he said mildly, his tone neutral but somehow still warm. "It's just an introduction. I didn't get to meet you like the other residents."

From someone else that would have sounded passive aggressive. From him, it came across as oddly sincere.

"I'm sorry for being late, Dr. Allende," she apologized.

"Happens to us all."

Before she could blink at that, he picked up a file and opened it.

"Dr. Romy Sasse, age twenty-nine, graduated top of your class at Stamford, did your internship and part of your residency at Johns Hopkins ... why transfer here for your last year? Johns Hopkins was very reluctant to let you go; we had to fight for you."

Old memories made her cold inside. "I had to come home to Seattle. Personal reasons. Also, my mother is getting married, rather unexpectedly."

"And she needs you to be here?"

Romy hesitated. "No, it's not that, but ..."

"But what?"

Romy sighed. It was none of his business, but she owed him this much after being late. "My sisters, Juno and Artemis, asked me to come. I'm the middle sister, the peacemaker. They have some concerns about Mom's fiancé."

"Really?" Blue looked interested, even though Romy couldn't for the life of her figure out why. Or why she just kept talking.

"It's not that he's a bad person, though I still haven't officially met him yet. But he's so entirely not what we thought Mom would go for ..." Abruptly, she halted, catching herself in mid-ramble. "I'm sorry, you really don't need to know this."

"No, please go on."

Romy frowned. "Well, then, you should know, my mom is a free spirit, a rainbow child, a hippie. Look at our names."

Blue smiled. "Okay, so Juno and Artemis, I get, but Romy?"

"Short for Romulus. Yes, I know it's technically a boy's name but, you see, I was a twin. Fraternal. My brother, Remy—Remus—died when we were five years old." God, the pain of it still haunted Romy. "Mom thought I was a boy too when she was pregnant, hence the name."

"So your name is actually Romulus?"

She was grateful he didn't press her for more details about Remy. "No, she managed to change it at the last moment on the birth certificate. Romy is my legal name."

"And you don't like your future stepfather?"

"I don't know him."

Suddenly Blue grinned. "I think your mom and Stuart Eames will be just fine."

Romy gaped at him in astonishment. "How the hell ...?"

He laughed, and his face looked even more desperately handsome than ever. "Believe it or not, I wasn't interrogating you without an actual purpose. You see, Romy Sasse, Stuart Eames is my father. So, technically, we're about to be siblings. Welcome to the family, Romy."

CHAPTER 2

Romy was still shell-shocked when she went to her mother's house that evening. Part of it was admittedly from the additional time she'd spent giddily talking in Blue's office —he'd insisted she call him that—and the rest was entirely due to his revelation.

"Why didn't you tell me Stuart was Blue Allende's father?"

Magda Sasse looked up from the cutting board and grinned at her middle daughter's abrupt greeting. "Hello to you, too. Because, dear one, Blue said he didn't want you to know right away. He wanted you to be on his service and thought you might not want to if you knew. Your reputation as a first-class doctor precedes you, honey, and I'm very proud."

Romy smiled and hugged her mother. "Thank you, Momma Bear. Anyway, Blue told me he will be with us for Thanksgiving?" Upon hearing that, she'd been hard-pressed to keep it together in the surgeon's office. Blue in her home, having dinner with her family ... why was that weirdly hot?

"Will it be awkward?" her mother asked in concern.

Romy hoisted herself up onto the kitchen counter and stole a piece of bell pepper Magda was slicing for salad. "I don't think so. Well, at least I hope not. He's a pretty even-tempered guy."

Magda smiled. "You like him?"

God, yes. He's the sexiest man I've ever met.

"Yeah, he's nice."

Nice was an understatement.

"He's an incredible surgeon. Watching him is like watching a maestro at work."

"Speaking of maestros." Magda often changed the direction of conversations on a whim, so Romy wasn't fazed. "Your sister has a new job. She's going to work for Livia's foundation as a lecturer."

Romy's eyebrows shot up. "She is? Juno's moving out?"

Her youngest sister, Juno, was the sister who most resembled their free-spirited mother. Tall and willowy, with a shock of messy blonde hair, and a confirmed tomboy, Juno Sasse had made music her first love and passion from a young age. She was the cherished baby of the family and Romy had half-suspected she'd never leave.

"She is," Magda confirmed, a touch of melancholy in her voice. Eternally supportive of her daughters though she was, Romy knew her mother would struggle with empty nest syndrome. "Although I'm trying desperately not to think about that day. She's starting in the New Year, so at least we'll have Christmas as a family."

"With Stuart's family too?"

Magda shot her a nervous look. "Well, yes. If that's okay with you and Arti."

"Why wouldn't it be?" Romy asked.

Magda sighed. "There is some, how can I put it, some unpleasantness with Stuart's wife. Hopefully soon to be ex-wife, if she ever signs the damn papers. She keeps harassing Stuart, usually through her son."

Romy raised an eyebrow, not liking the sound of that. "What's the son's name again?"

"Gaius. I've only met him once, but he seems friendly enough. Hasn't Blue ever mentioned him?"

"We're careful to keep family stuff away from work, and I don't actually socialize with Blue Allende, remember? We'd never even met until today. He might be my brother soon, but he's still in a league of his own." Romy grinned as Magda rolled her eyes.

"You mean you don't socialize *at all*. Romy, you're beautiful, you're young ... don't let what happened in New York stop you from living your life."

Romy grimaced, feeling the familiar cold feeling at the memories. "Mom ... Dacre doesn't know I'm back home, and if he finds out, he'll come here and ... God, I don't want to imagine."

Her mother looked down at her hands as they continued to move swiftly, her knife skills in the kitchen as good as any surgeon's were in an operating theater. "I hate that you were with him. You're too young to have gone through a divorce or anything else he did to you."

Romy marshalled her emotions, reminding herself that those days were long past. She was safe now, however much Dacre Mortimer was an animal. Her leg still hurt from where he'd stamped on it and broken it the previous year at the same time that he'd almost beaten her to death.

"Look, at least I learned a lesson," Romy said to her mother now. "Don't go on first impressions. Dacre was Mr. Charm until he *wasn't*."

"Was that a dig at me?" Magda didn't sound upset, just sad. "Because I know Stuart and I haven't known each other that long."

Romy hopped down to kiss her mother's cheek and gave her a warm hug.

"Mom, no, it wasn't a dig at you, more one at myself."

Magda smiled in relief. "Romy, I have never felt like this. Not even with your father," she added apologetically.

"I figured, with Dad." Romy nodded, unsurprised.

Romy's father, a professor of Magda's back in the day, had never been present much in his daughters' lives. He supported them financially, but soon after Juno had been born, he and Magda had quietly and amicably divorced and James Sasse had remarried and moved to London. Being a single mother didn't faze Magda and she'd somehow kept her girls clothed and fed as they grew, bringing them all up to be independent young people who never depended on someone else.

The loss of Remy, Romy's brother, had shattered them all, but the four women were as close now as they had ever been. Artemis, Magda's eldest, had followed her father into the teaching profession and now taught physics at the University of Washington. Romy had headed for medical school as soon as she graduated from Harvard, and Juno was a musical prodigy. The one thing James had provided was money for their education, and Magda was grateful for that, she often told Romy.

Magda had been brought up in a hippie commune and she'd carried those values her whole life, finally having reached a point in her life where she could sculpt for a living.

Which was why Romy and her sisters had been astounded to hear that Magda was about to marry a multi-billionaire. Stuart Eames had made his fortune in tech and had such a large share of the tech market that no one could compete. Romy was looking forward to meeting the billionaire who had captured her mother's laidback heart.

A random thought occurred to her as she reached for the salad bowl and started to assemble the various ingredients her mother had diced. "How come Blue has a different last name?"

Magda drained the pot of rice she was cooking. "He's Stuart's son from an affair."

Romy's eyebrows shot up.

"I think his mother was Italian," Magda went on, confirming at least that suspicion, though Romy was far more interested in the other revelation.

"So ... Stuart had an affair?"

Magda gave her a warning look. "Darling, if you had ever met his wife, you wouldn't blame him."

Though Magda was far from conservative, she was fiercely loyal and it was an unusual stance for her to take. Nevertheless, Romy decided to let it go, at least until she'd had a chance to cross-examine Eames and ensure that he wasn't about to cheat on her mother. Because if he did, she and her sisters would have plenty to say.

"Mom," she said, suddenly noticing how much food her mother was preparing, "you realize there's only four of us, right?"

"Five," Magda flushed bright red and ducked her head. "Stuart's joining us."

"Oh, getting in an introduction under the wire, huh?" Romy grinned. "I guess I should help you with the rest of dinner, then ..."

STUART EAMES HAD the same bright green eyes as his son, but his hair was close cropped and white. He had an easy smile that Romy liked, and a friendly manner which made the party all feel at ease. He greeted them all with utmost respect. "It's so good to finally meet you. Magda is so proud of you all."

Juno, curling herself into a chair, grinned at him. "I assure you, we don't deserve it."

Artemis, her blonde hair falling gracefully to her shoulders, shot her younger sister a warning look. "Don't tease, Juno."

Stuart laughed. "No, don't stop teasing. Blue and I are always busting each other's chops. It's what families are supposed to do. Speaking of which, do you mind if I just have a quiet word with your mom about something? I swear it'll take no more than five minutes."

"Sure thing."

Left alone, the sisters looked at one another.

"He's cute," Juno decided, and Artemis chuckled.

"Can you call a sixty-year-old cute?" Artemis smoothed her skirt down over her long legs, crossing them elegantly.

Romy sighed. Of all the Sasse sisters, she was the odd one out, dark-haired, dark eyed, and small in stature, if not in figure. Where her sisters were all long limbs and athletic, Romy was curvy, full-breasted, and petite. She still worked out as much as her siblings, but her figure was always going to be soft instead of athletic like them. Juno and Artemis took after their mother; Romy didn't know where she'd gotten her curves from. She barely remembered what her father looked like. Oh, she knew people considered her beautiful, but she never played it up. Slightly myopic from a young age, she wore glasses instead of contacts, and stuffed her long, thick chestnut hair up into a messy bun more often than not.

Juno poked her with a foot now. "Will you be coming to our traditional Thanksgiving run this year?"

Giving her sister a cheesy smile, Romy said, "Sadly, I'll be working."

"Roms!"

"Sorry," Romy sang in a not-so-at-all voice. She loathed running, unless it was towards something. Like pizza.

Juno sulked while Artemis grinned at Romy. "Nice work, Romy. And what with my broken ankle ..."

"What broken ankle?" Juno shot her eldest sister a confused look.

"The one I'll mysteriously acquire on Thanksgiving." Artemis laughed and high-fived Romy.

"Don't blame me when the pair of you get old and fat." Juno sighed dramatically, then, lowering her voice, she nodded towards the kitchen where Stuart and their mother talking. "What do you think?"

"Too early to say."

"He looks like Blue a little. Same eyes."

Juno grinned. "You got a little crush, Romulus?"

Romy threw a pillow at her. "None of your business, quisling."

Dinner was a fun affair, and Romy decided she liked Stuart very much. He was charming, intelligent, and seemed to adore her mother. Romy noticed, however, that Artemis was a little quieter than normal and when she questioned her sister afterward, Artemis shrugged.

"I'm just reserving judgement is all, Romy. We don't know him that well yet."

Romy went to work the next day, wondering if she should mention Stuart to Blue, but when she walked into the locker room, the place was in a chaotic state with people running every which way.

"What's going on?" she asked, preparing herself mentally and physically for what would likely be a long haul.

"There's been an attack at a sorority house," Mac told her, his face pale. "Really nasty stuff. Eight girls, three dead. The rest are being brought in here. Allende is already operating."

Every time she thought she was used to the darker side of her profession, Romy got a reality check. Because truthfully, there was no way to ever get used to innocents slaughtered.

Reaching for her scrubs automatically, she asked, "Does he want us in the observation room?"

"No." They heard Blue's voice behind them and turned. Clad in bloodstained scrubs, the handsome surgeon looked weary and grim-faced. "Romy, you're with me in OR3; Mac, with Dr. Fredericks in OR7; Jim, Molly, and Flynn, emergency room until we can find theaters for the less injured girls. Come on, Romy."

She changed and was back in under a minute. Blue briefed her on the way to theater. "Patient is Yasmin Levant, nineteen, multiple stab wounds to the abdomen, shattered left femur, looks like the killer stamped on it, possibly to incapacitate her. We've got Ortho coming in but her abdominal wounds are catastrophic, at least twenty-nine separate wounds."

"God, poor girl."

Blue nodded as they went to scrub. "Look, Romy, we're going to do everything and anything to save her, but I have to warn you. The odds are against us."

She'd expected as much, sadly, but appreciated the warning anyway.

After scrubbing, Romy followed him into the operating room where the victim lay on the table. She was covered in blood and barely breathing, blood bags and saline trying to keep her alive. Automatically, Romy avoided looking at anything but the injuries. Looking at the faces right off the bat when the situation was so dire … it didn't help things.

For hours they operated, trying to repair the damage the knife had caused, pumping her full of blood, but at midnight, Blue called it. There was nothing else to do …

Yasmin Levant was dead.

CHAPTER 3

The adrenaline leaving her system, Romy felt weirdly emotional, horrified, and drained by the experience. She waited until almost everyone had left the room before walking up to Yasmin's head. Finally looking at the young girl's still, pale face, her dark hair blood-soaked to an auburn color, Romy saw herself reflected in the victim's silent, still features. She whispered a silent apology for her failure and started removing the tubes from her throat.

"The nurses will do that," Blue said gently, putting his hand on her back. Romy, unable to speak, just shook her head and eventually Blue began to help her, both working in silence until all the medical equipment had been cleared away and Yasmin lay on the table silent and still, but at least with slightly more dignity.

"Can I wash her face?" Romy found her voice breaking as she asked, but Blue, his eyes sad, shook his head.

"No, we have to keep her secure for the forensic team now. Even all of our equipment will need to be saved. The police will probably want a statement from all of us."

Romy looked back down at Yasmin and a sob choked its way out of her. "Who would do this? Why?"

She felt Blue draw her away from the victim then and wrap his arms around her. It wasn't what colleagues usually did, but Romy allowed it because she needed it. She leaned into him, tears filling her eyes.

"I wish I could tell you it gets easier in these cases, Romy, but it doesn't," he said softly, his voice achingly sad and kind. "The vile things people do to other humans—sometimes there is no reason why. Sometimes people are monsters."

Romy nodded and looked up at him, wiping her eyes. "I know the type."

Blue stopped, and his green eyes were intense on hers. For a long moment they gazed at each other before, blushing, Romy gave an awkward smile and stepped away. "I'm okay now. We'd better go talk to the family."

"Of course." There was pain in that beautiful voice of his and Romy wanted to hold him and comfort him as he had done with her, but Blue walked away. She followed him, running slightly to keep up with his long stride. He dwarfed her five-foot two by at least a foot, and suddenly he slowed down. "Sorry, *piccolo*, I'll try not to walk so fast."

"*Piccolo*?"

"*Little one*," he explained, the tenderness in his voice tugging at her heart as much as the hint of a smile. Then as they neared the relative's room, his smile faded. "Is this your first one?"

"First murder." Romy's heart began to beat out of her chest.

Blue nodded, squeezing her hand. "Just follow my lead."

They knocked and walked in. A middle-aged woman, terrified, was sitting down, her arms wrapped around herself, and when she saw their faces, she moaned. "*No, no, no, no...*"

A man, her husband, his face etched with pain, stood. "Doc? Please don't tell me ..."

"I'm so sorry, Mr. and Mrs. Levant. Despite our best efforts, Yasmin's injuries were too severe and she died a short time ago."

The woman collapsed in a sobbing, weeping huddle, and Blue

kept talking to her husband as Romy moved to try and comfort Yasmin's mother.

"There are no words for the regret I feel, *we* feel, at your loss."

Trying futilely to soothe the mother's unsoothable grief, Romy listened to Blue talk first to Yasmin's father, then watched him take a turn gently addressing her bereft mother, comforting both as best as he could, answering all of their questions patiently and as fully as possible. But the truth was the one question would never be adequately answered.

Why?

Romy's chest was tight with sorrow but she maintained her composure. Afterward, they talked to the police, those questions prolonging the endless night even further. Finally, as dawn began to break over Seattle, Romy went back to the locker room to change out of her bloody scrubs. The room was empty and echoed with each footstep and slam of the locker door.

Somehow managing to drag on her jeans and shirt, Romy slumped onto a bench afterward and put her head in her hands. The adrenaline from the surgery was long gone and now she felt wrecked. Her hip and leg ached from standing too long but she ignored the pain, trying not to break down. She failed, and silent, hot tears poured down her face. She buried her face in her hands to cry, her entire body trembling.

She heard him come in; it was impossible not to in the silence, but she didn't expect to feel his arms go around her for the second time that evening. Gently, he drew her head to his chest. His clean soap-and-spice smell was familiar now and Romy pressed her face into his sweater, breathing him in. He stroked her hair and whispered soft Italian words, resting his chin on her head and just letting her weep.

When she finally stopped crying, she looked up at him. His eyes were sad, but he held her gaze for a moment before brushing his lips against hers just briefly. It was clear from the look on his face that he'd intended it as no more than a reassurance, but the heat that instantly flared between them changed those intentions. They both felt it, so there was not even the slightest chance of denying the chemistry.

Blue framed her face with his big hands. "Are you sure, Romy?" His voice was low and sent shivers of desire through her body.

"It is wrong?" she whispered, looking up into his intensely compassionate eyes. "She just died. How can we ..."

"Life has to go on, *piccolo*," he said softly. "We honor those who go before us by continuing to live fully. But if you prefer not to, I understand absolutely—"

"No. Yes." Romy slid her hand into his dark curls and kissed him hard, needing this. Needing him. Their mouths moved together hungrily, and when Blue stood and picked her up, it was like she belonged in his careful embrace. He carried her as if she weighed nothing, kicking open the door to the on-call room and locking it behind him.

He set her down on her feet and gently pulled at the drawstring of her pants, drawing them down her legs then pulling her top over her head. "God, you're beautiful," he said softly, and she could see the lust and admiration in his eyes. Her own hands went down to his groin, cupping his hard-on through his jeans. Damn, he was huge ...

Blue pulled down the lacy cup of her bra and fixed his mouth on her nipple as he slid her panties down her legs, then expertly flicked her bra clasp open, letting her full, ripe breasts fall into his hands. The feel of his skin on hers was sending tingles racing through her body and she pushed his sweater over his head and ran her hands over the hard planes of his chest. Naked, Blue Allende was even more godlike, tall, broad-shouldered, and slim-hipped. He swept her onto the small bunk, kissing her as he kicked off his pants and underwear. Romy reached down to stroke his cock, the skin so silky, the hard, hot length of him filling her hands.

Blue was kissing her breasts, her belly, as he made his way down the bed and hooked her legs over his shoulders. He smiled up at her. "I'm going to lick you until you scream, beautiful girl ..."

Romy moaned, drawing in a sharp breath as his tongue lashed

around her clit, his fingers massaging the soft flesh of her inner thigh as he expertly pleasured her. "God, Blue ... Blue ..."

A rush of emotion flooded her system as she came and she began to cry, much to her embarrassment. His mouth was on hers then, tender, loving. "Don't cry, *piccolo*," he murmured, his eyes soft. Romy stroked his face but said nothing, drinking him in.

"Do you want me inside?"

She nodded and as she watched him slip a condom onto his straining cock, Romy knew she had wanted this man from the first moment she had seen him.

Blue hitched her legs around his waist. "Okay?"

She nodded and he smiled, pausing to stroke her belly, before she helped guide him into her. With one long thrust, he entered her, and Romy gasped with the thrill of him filling her, the rhythm that he found so quickly. She moved with him, meeting and holding his gaze until they were both trembling and panting for air. She tightened her vaginal muscles around his pulsating cock, making him groan her name. And as she came, her back arched up and she cried out as he kissed her throat, her breasts.

Afterward, he held her as she tried to stop her body trembling, kissing her forehead and the tears that still lingered at the corners of her eyes from the emotion of everything. "Are you okay, *piccolo*?"

She nodded, stroking his face. "I am very, very okay. Surprisingly so. Should we have done that?"

Blue smiled wryly. "Probably not ... but I admit, I've wanted to do that since I first met you."

Romy was amazed. "*Me*?"

He laughed. "Yes, why is that hard to believe? You're beautiful, smart, funny, the whole package. Who *wouldn't* want you?"

"But you could have anyone you want, Blue. Anyone."

"And I want you, Romy." He sighed. "Although I'm not naïve that this will be complicated, not just at work, but with our families."

Romy groaned. "I didn't even think about that ... God. Maybe we should keep this," she gestured to their naked bodies, "to ourselves."

Blue nodded, then grinned at her. "I'd like to keep your body all to myself."

Romy laughed as he covered her body with his, feeling his cock hardening again. "I'm serious."

"Secret liaisons? That's pretty hot." He kissed her neck, then moved again to her lips. "I can't get enough of these lips."

She smiled, her mouth curving up as he kissed her, but when he broke away, her eyes were serious. "This is so complicated, Blue. You're my boss to begin with, then there's our families. I mean it. We should keep this between us ... assuming, um, assuming this isn't a one-night thing." She blushed again, but he laughed.

"It isn't, not for me, but I do agree with you. Maybe next time we'll keep it out of the hospital, but tonight, heightened emotions, I needed this. I needed you."

Touched, she cupped his cheek in her hand. "You have me. Just ... on the down-low. I can't risk my career, Blue, as much as I want you."

"I agree, Romy." He sighed and leaned his forehead against hers. "And I hate to do this, but I have to be back on rounds in three hours and so do you."

"Yeah, we'd better go home. I mean to our *own* homes," she added, smiling as he chuckled.

Somehow they managed to keep their hands off one another long enough to get dressed and walk outside.

Down in the parking lot, he stole one more kiss. "You're heavenly," he said quietly, but with intensity in his eyes. "I'll see you in a few hours. Take some time. I'll cover for you."

Romy saw him watching her car as she drove away, her emotions in turmoil. The man knew how to make her body respond like no one ever had. More than that, he seemed to see something in her that she'd thought Dacre's assault had stamped out permanently. There was a goodness to Blue, a tenderness to where it wasn't just red-hot searing sex but also something more, even this very first time.

She wasn't sure she'd be able to keep the secret, but it was sure worth giving it a damn good try.

CHAPTER 4

A t home, Romy set an alarm for two hours and fell onto her bed still fully clothed. She groaned when the alarm went off and hauled herself out of bed, finally discarding her work clothes and stepping into the shower. As she ate a quick breakfast, she flicked on the television and watched the reports of the murders. It was an awful idea but she needed to see it somehow, as though it helped atone slightly for being unable to save Yasmin. As thought it might help her understand even slightly.

THE FOUR DECEASED YOUNG WOMEN, *savagely attacked in their sorority house, have now been named as Rebecca Fulsome, 20; Oona White, 19; Madelaine Culpepper, 21; and the youngest victim, Yasmin Levant, who at just 18, died last night of her wounds at The Rainier Hope Hospital. Hospital officials say that their best surgeons worked tirelessly to save Miss Levant, but she succumbed to her injuries in the early hours of this morning. Police say the attacker broke in through an open window and attacked each girl in her bedroom, before leaving the premises. So far, no suspects have been identified, but the murders mirror a similar case in New York two years ago.*

. . .

ROMY SWALLOWED the last of her cereal, feeling sick. She'd forgotten all about the murders in New York. God, there were monsters everywhere. She remembered her own personal monster, the midnight beatings, the forced sex.

Rape. Call it what it was, Sasse. He raped you. Bastard.

She drove into work and was assailed by her friends, wanting to know about working with Blue in an emergency situation. Romy, exhausted, was grateful when Mac rescued her, shooing everyone away and bearing her off to the cafeteria. "Allende sent me. He saw you come in and knew you'd get caught by the pack. Damn hyenas."

Romy smiled at him and at Blue's thoughtfulness. "Mac, if it had been someone else but me, we would have been hyenas too."

Mac shrugged. "Fair point. Are you okay? You look done in."

"It was a long night." In more ways than one. "Is Dr. Allende all right? He had it worse than me."

"He looks good, but then he always does."

"True story."

Mac grinned at her. "So you're not immune to the good doctor's charisma then? I thought you were the one hold-out."

Romy cursed silently but faked a smile. "I'm here to work, not get laid."

"I'm just saying ... out of all us, I reckon you'd be his type."

Romy shrugged off the conversation. "Did you hear the news this morning? The murders in New York? The same as here?"

"Yeah. Jesus, humans, huh?"

"Humans." She agreed. Her pager went off a second before Mac's. "We're summoned."

IT WAS evening before she even saw Blue again. There was so much paperwork from the murders and the subsequent medical procedures that Romy was sequestered with a police team most of the day.

They went over everything again and again. Romy told them again how Yasmin Levant had been stabbed so viciously that her abdominal artery had been shredded, that she had simply bled out before they could attempt any kind of repair.

"What about her left femur?" Det. Halsey asked her eventually. "Did your orthopedic department attend the surgery?"

Romy nodded. "But, to be honest, it was secondary to the abdominal wounds. I'm not an expert, but I assume he—or she—broke her femur to subdue her enough that she couldn't fight him—or her —off."

"We're pretty sure it's a him," Halsey said quietly.

Romy, overtired bristled. "Because women aren't strong enough to do that to a person?"

Halsey held his hands up. "I meant no offense, Dr. Sasse. We found DNA on the victim. Male DNA."

Romy backed down. "I'm sorry. Bad day."

"Of course. Look, we need to talk about the survivors' injuries. We got the report that they weren't as serious as the deceased victims."

"No, that was strange," Romy said. "They were badly beaten, and they'll probably need serious psychiatric counseling, but yeah, it is odd that he didn't finish the job, so to speak. God."

"And Ms. Levant was the only one with a broken femur?"

Romy's own leg ached and she rubbed it unconsciously. "Detective, the femur is the longest, strongest bone in the human body. The force it takes to break it ... it would take anger. Rage. It's sadistic too ... but then, that's what we're talking about here, isn't it? He's a sadist."

"He is," the detective agreed, then smiled kindly at her. "You'll tell your friends to be careful when they leave at night?"

Romy gave a hollow laugh. "Detective, you're talking about everyday life for a woman in this world."

NOT EVEN HALFWAY THROUGH her shift, Romy was hollowed out through and through. She didn't know if she even had the strength to walk out of the hospital for a breath of fresh air, when Blue appeared in the breakroom. He didn't say a word, helping himself to coffee nonchalantly before stepping into the supply closet.

She knew he was giving her a chance to choose, and choose she did. Dragging herself out of her seat, she joined him in the small room and locked the door.

"This isn't 'keeping it out of work' Dr. Allende."

Blue reached for her. "Shut up and kiss me, woman."

He crushed his lips against hers, his arms snaking around her waist, pulling her hard against his body. Romy moaned as she felt his erection, hard against her belly. For just a moment she let herself sag, let him carry her weary weight ... "God, I want you, but ..."

Reality reasserted itself and gently she extricated herself from his arms. "Bad boy." She wagged her finger at him and he laughed.

"Come home with me tonight and I'll show you just how much of a bad boy I can be."

Romy hesitated, but then the lure of his green eyes, his dark curls and that body ...

"*Piccolo*, unless you want to sleep," he said softly, studying her face and holding her more gently. "No pressure, you understand. It's been a long two days. Another day, if you prefer ..."

"No." Romy made up her mind. *The best way to honor those who have gone before us is to continue living our lives fully.* "I'm off tomorrow, so I can risk it."

Blue flashed a huge grin. "Oh, you're off tomorrow ... funny thing ... so am I."

Romy started laughing. "I wonder how that happened?"

"Come here."

They kissed again, and Romy reached down to squeeze his diamond-hard cock. He groaned and buried his face in her neck. "It's a good thing we're off, because I'm going to make sure you can't walk straight for the entire day."

"Is that right?"

"God, yes."

Romy giggled as he pretended to ravish her. "Easy, soldier. You're the one who's not going to be able to walk properly, and we still have rounds."

"Spoilsport."

"Get over it, Doc."

ROMY'S BODY felt electrified all day at the thought of what Blue had promised. That electricity gave her a much-needed boost that, paired with caffeine, got her through the remainder of the long hours. But as the day wound down and she walked down to the concessions stand to grab a new toothbrush, she groaned inwardly as she saw a tall, blonde, and very familiar figure looping towards her.

"Yo, sis." Juno grinned, flinging her long arms around her diminutive sister.

"Hey, Boo ... what are you doing here?"

"Just finished a class and wanted to say hi. Also, to check out the famous doc ... is he here?"

Romy opened her mouth to answer just as Blue came toward her, grinning. She gave a quick, almost imperceptible shake of the head, and cut her eyes to Juno. Blue slowed his pace, his smile faltering in confusion.

"Dr. Allende, do you have a moment?" Romy said formally. "My sister Juno would like to meet you."

Understanding now, Blue smiled at Juno, shaking her hand. "Hey, nice to meet you at last."

"You too." Juno's amazed expression was written all over her face as she took in the gorgeous man. "Can I call you Blue?"

"Of course. Listen, would you ladies like to grab a coffee?"

Romy was gesturing wildly behind Juno's back, but Blue didn't understand her signal, and when Juno agreed—a little too enthusiastically—Romy sighed. She knew Juno—any excuse to stay at Romy's place overnight in the city, especially if there was a chance to gossip. *Damn it.*

They went for a coffee at a little independent place on 6th Avenue. Blue smiled at Juno. "So, we're about to be siblings?"

"Looks like." Juno was stuffing a Danish pastry into her mouth. "We haven't met your brother yet, either. Mom's looking forward to Thanksgiving dinner—just a warning, she cooks brussels sprouts, and given it's ..." she checked her watch, "two weeks until Thanksgiving, she'll be putting them on to boil about now."

Blue laughed. "Duly noted. Dad and I are looking forward to spending that day with you."

"And your brother?"

There was a pause, a beat too long. "And Gaius. Of course."

"You don't mention your brother much," Romy said and saw a flicker of something in his eyes before he gave them a half-smile.

"We're not as close as you three appear to be. I always wanted a sister. Juno, Romy tells me you're quite the musical prodigy."

"Ha." Juno grinned at him. "She flatters me. But it is my passion, and I'm about to start working for the Gabriella Renaud Foundation down in New Orleans."

"Just when I move back to Seattle, she moves out," Romy grinned. "I might take it personally."

"Then you'll have to make the most of me while I'm here. Like tonight ... I could stay over at your place?" Juno looked hopeful, and Romy had to work to keep the disappointment out of her face.

"Of course, Boo." She shot an apologetic look at Blue who winked at her and mouthed 'don't worry' at her. "But," Romy added, thinking quickly, "I have to be out early tomorrow for a training seminar. All day, I'm afraid."

"Yes, she does," Blue caught on, trying not to smile. "I'm leading that seminar, and I'm very strict about time. One of my things, I'm afraid, punctuality."

"He is."

Juno shrugged, surprisingly clueless. Usually she picked up on these things with a terrifying radar. "What's the training about?"

"Orthopedics," Blue said smoothly, "mostly about the recovery time of someone's gait after strenuous exercise."

Romy snorted her coffee from her nose and was embarrassed, wiping her nose. "Sorry, went down the wrong way."

"That's not like you," Blue said innocently, and Romy had to hide her laughter in her tissue. Juno still didn't notice anything, already making inroads on Romy's carrot cake, which she'd left alone. Romy, trying to stop her giggles, cleared her throat.

"So, yeah, if you don't mind being left alone in the apartment."

"Of course not." Juno shrugged.

Blue's eyes were twinkling. "Don't forget we also have that patient we might need to check in on overnight too. I'll page you if I need you."

"Please do," Romy was enjoying their little game, "I'd like to make sure the patient is, um, responding to stimulus."

It was Blue's turn to hide his laughter now. "Do excuse me, I have to use the bathroom."

When they were alone, Juno turned to Romy. "Well, he's gorgeous and sweet and cute. How do you concentrate on work with a man like that around?"

"A man who will soon be our brother," Romy reminded her, cringing inwardly. She hated lying to Juno, who was so trusting that she would believe anything Romy told her. "Also, he's my boss."

"Ha, flirty boss." But Juno didn't push it. She gave up on the carrot cake, licking cream cheese frosting from her fingers. "Look, maybe I will go home tonight. Seems like you're preoccupied with work anyway. But we must, must, must have a sisters' night before I leave for New Orleans."

"Are you going before Christmas?" For some reason, Romy was confused about the timeline. Had Juno told her and she'd just forgotten?

"Only for a couple of weeks, just so Livia can get me trained before she gives birth. Can you believe she's having a baby?"

"I'm just glad she's well enough to." Their friend Livia had been stabbed and shot by a psychopath the year before and had barely survived. "Give her and Nox my love, won't you?"

"Speaking of gorgeous men." Juno muttered, then grinned as Blue returned. "It was so good to meet you, bro, but I think I'm going to head back home, leave you your second-in-command." She threw her arms around his neck and hugged him. Faintly surprised, Blue smiled and returned the embrace. "You're coming to Thanksgiving, right?"

Blue nodded. "Just try and stop me. I'm a sucker for over-boiled sprouts."

Laughing, Juno kissed Romy's cheek and then loped out, garnering the appreciative looks of a table of young men as she walked out of the coffee house.

Blue grinned at Romy. "So ... you're free, after all?" He sat down next to her and slid his hand along her thigh. Romy wiggled with pleasure.

"Dr. Allende?"

"Yes, Dr. Sasse?"

"I believe you prescribed me some bone-shattering sex earlier ... how about you fill my prescription?"

Blue laughed. "That was the worst doctor dirty talk I've ever heard ... but yes, I need to do that immediately ..."

GAIUS EAMES TAPPED on his father's office door, not waiting for a reply before he opened it. "Hey, Pa."

Stuart looked up over from his computer, annoyed. "Gaius, why bother to knock if you're just going to come in anyway?"

Gaius was unrepentant, shrugging as he flopped into the chair opposite his father. "I just get into town and that's the greeting I get? What would I have caught you doing? One of your secretaries?"

"That's enough, Gaius." Stuart glared at his eldest son.

Gaius grinned widely, knowing his barb had hit home. "*Jeez*, Pa, take a chill pill. I was *kidding*. How is the lovely Magda?"

Stuart's face softened. "She's wonderful, and looking forward to seeing you at Thanksgiving —you are coming, I take it?"

Gaius nodded. "Although Mom's not happy, yes, I'll be there."

Stuart sighed. "At this point, I really don't care what Hilary thinks anymore, Gaius. She burned her bridges long ago."

"I don't want to fight, Pa." Gaius held his hands up. "So, Thanksgiving. Will I meet the daughters? I've done my research, two blondes, one brunette —have they got the same father? I'm just asking," he added as his father looked annoyed, "no judgement."

"As far as I know, yes. Artemis and Juno take after Magda, and Romy after her father, I understand. Anyway, you'll meet all of them then. Have you spoken ..."

"To the Italian?" Gaius finished his father's sentence. "No, but then that's nothing new."

Stuart sighed. "Blue is your brother, Gaius, and it's about time you both grew up."

Gaius stayed silent. He would never, ever bond with Blue Allende, and not just because he was his bastard half-brother. The jealous that squirmed in his gut when he thought about Blue's success, his devastating good looks, his decency ... goddamn.

"I hear he's working with one of the Sasse girls."

Stuart nodded. "Romy. She's in her last year of residency. Blue says she's the best he's ever seen."

Gaius chuckled darkly. "Is he fucking her?"

Stuart's blue eyes went gray, and Gaius knew he'd gone too far this time. "Don't ever talk about one of Magda's daughters like that again. Ever."

"Forgive me." Gaius tried to keep the sarcasm out of his voice. "Look, I just got into town —can I use the condo? I'm assuming you've moved in with Magda already?"

"Close enough. I spend every night there. Here," Stuart reached into his desk drawer and threw Gaius a set of keys. "You know the rules."

"Pa, you realize I'm forty-two, right?"

"And Charlie Sheen is fifty-something. No whores, no drugs. Not in my condo."

Gaius sighed and got up. "Fine. Well, I guess I'll see you at Thanksgiving."

Stuart relented a little. The man had a soft spot that made Gaius respect him even less. "Look, have dinner with me, just me, on Tuesday."

Gaius masked a smirk. "It's a date."

AT HIS FATHER'S CONDO, Gaius unpacked, then grabbed a beer from the refrigerator and stretched out on the couch, flicking through the television channels disinterestedly. It was gnawing at his gut the way his father talked about Blue, the pride, the love in his voice. Gaius had been seventeen when his father had revealed his affair with Blue's mother. He hadn't blame his father for straying—he knew his own mother Hilary hadn't been faithful at any point during his parents' marriage, but he'd resented the fact that there was a child.

Blue, twelve at the time that his father brought him into their family, was quiet, kind, intense, and everything Gaius wanted to be. Even as a child, Blue's big green eyes, full of intelligence and compassion, garnered him quick acceptance into their family circle, something Gaius had struggled with. However much Blue had tried to befriend his new brother, Gaius, ridden by jealousy, had been uninterested.

Gaius gave a humorless laugh. Now Blue already had an 'in' with his father's new wife and her daughters too. *Fuck him.* Gaius grabbed his iPad and typed in a name in the search engine.

Doctor Romy Sasse. Her photograph came up immediately on the alumni page at Stamford's website, and Gaius studied it. Long, dark hair falling in waves past her shoulders, Romy was a doe-eyed beauty with her olive skin, that faint blush of pink in her cheeks, and the curve of her breasts in her white coat was promising.

Yeah, Gaius thought, if Blue isn't fucking her, *he's a fool.* Gaius read everything he could on the young woman, but there was a surprising dearth of information. Weren't doctors always publishing research? Why were her name and profile not on the website of the Rainier Hope Hospital, but only on the alumni page of Stamford? Did she not want people to know where she was?

Intrigued, Gaius took out his phone and dialed. "Yeah, Greg? It's Gaius Eames. Yes, good, thanks. Listen, I have a job for you, if you're interested. Yeah, I want you to find out everything you can on a Dr. Romy Sasse. She's a resident at Rainier Hope Hospital. Find out what she's hiding ... or who she's hiding from."

CHAPTER 5

At the same moment that Gaius set out to find out more about Romy, his half-brother was doing the same thing—albeit in a more physical way. He trailed his lips up the length of her spine, feeling her shiver. Her skin was so soft that it drove him crazy. "Turn over, baby."

Romy rolled onto her back, hitching a leg over his body. Her lips crushed against his as he buried his rock-hard cock deep into her, and he heard her moan of pleasure. He couldn't get enough of this woman; she was so soft, her skin silky, the color of milky coffee. The way she looked up at him with those dark chocolate eyes ...

He found his rhythm, moving in and out of her, feeling her sweet cunt contract around his cock, loving the way her breasts and belly undulated with the movement. He'd never been one for skinny girls and Romy had the kind of curvaceous body men salivated over. He'd wanted her the moment he saw her, and he hadn't felt that way in a long time.

Blue was aware that his physical attributes meant people thought he was a man whore, and he himself had done nothing to dissuade that image but the truth was ... he was careful with his heart. So many women wanted him to look good on their arm, or wanted his cachet as a superstar surgeon to show off. Very few wanted Blue for who he really was underneath the movie-star looks, a funny, unabashed geek, who just wanted to find someone to laugh with.

And very quickly after she'd arrived in Seattle, Romy had shown herself to be just that woman. That they would soon be related by marriage and be siblings, well, they'd have to deal with that later.

For now, all he wanted to do was make love to her. He stroked the hair back from her face as they moved together, marveling at the beautiful flush in her face as she came, trembling and sighing his name. They smiled at each other as they caught their breath.

"I've never had sex this good," Roy said, stretching her limbs and then curling into him.

For a long moment, Blue stared at her. "I wish we could go public," he said regretfully. "I want to tell the world about this brilliant, beautiful woman who somehow wants me."

Romy laughed. "First, thank you for complimenting my intellect first; you get extra points for that. Second, you know you could have any woman you wanted, Blue Allende. Don't be modest. You know it's the truth."

"It's the accent," he said playfully before letting loose with a string of Italian. "*Ho incontrato la ragazza più gloriosa e voglio portarla in tutte le mie parti preferite d'Italia e farle vedere da dove vengo.*"

"Holy crap, that's unfairly hot!" Romy exclaimed, kissing him hungrily.

"Ah, a weakness," he teased, tickling her ribs and enjoying her writhing against him.

"Mmm, *yeah.* Now ... what did you say? There was something about a ho and glorious ravioli?"

Blue grinned. "I just said I met the most glorious girl, and I want to take her to all my favorite parts of Italy and show her where I came from."

"Wow. Where *did* you come from?" she wondered. "I mean, I know Stuart had an affair with your mom ..." she trailed off, apparently realizing that wasn't the hottest of pillow talk conversations.

"He did," Blue nodded, long ago having come to terms with that aspect of his DNA.

"Technically he was—and regretfully still is—married to Hilary." Just mentioning her name made his gut tense for reasons no one knew but him. "But the marriage has been over for years. Mom was a widow; her husband was killed in a car wreck three years after they married, and she was in mourning for years. Stuart went to Rome for a conference, met my mother, and it was, according to her, like a thunderbolt."

Blue rolled over onto his back and gathered Romy back into him, enjoyed her pressed tight against his chest. "I was conceived on that first meeting, accidentally, of course, and my mom even gave Stuart an out, said she would raise me alone. Stuart was a stand-up guy. He and my mother ... their chemistry was plain to see even when I was a kid, so when my mom died, Stuart didn't hesitate to bring me to the States."

"That makes me very happy to hear," Romy nodded. "Not the affair, obviously, but it doesn't seem like he'll break my mom's heart."

"No," Blue assured her. "He will not, Romy. He made mistakes, yes, but he is a genuinely good man."

Romy's face clouded. "What is your stepmother like?"

"Hilary?" Blue gave a humorless laugh, feeling that wrench again. "Hilary Eames is an unremittingly vile piece of crap. Sorry if that sounds harsh, but it's the truth. She treated—and continues to treat —my dad as an ATM machine, but gives the world the impression she's a God-fearing charitable Christian woman. Ugh. That woman has never believed in anything in her life."

"She's that bad?"

Blue nodded. "Thankfully, Dad saw the light and filed for divorce, but it hasn't stopped her from trying to control him. And Dad's so desperate for the divorce to be final, he gives in on everything. She's bleeding him dry. I haven't met your mom yet, Romy, but I would warn her ..." he looked at her intensely, willing her to feel the depth of his warning, "don't let Hilary in, even an inch. She's like a cancer, and I haven't even told you the half of it."

Romy propped herself up on her elbow and studied him. "She won't get a chance, I promise. No one messes with my mom—they have to get past me and my sisters and we can throw down, I tell you."

Blue smiled fondly at her. "I bet you can. I really look forward to meeting Magda. She's made my dad happy, and I owe her everything for that."

"Thanksgiving."

There was a tiny pause before he nodded at the invitation. "Thanksgiving. Yes." He bent his head to kiss her. "Now, Romy, be a good girl and lie back for me ... I'm going to kiss every inch of your spectacular body."

Soon, he was hooking her legs over his shoulder and burying his face in her sex. She tasted so good to him, the crimson blush of her swollen cunt so beautiful as his tongue teased and tormented her hardening clit until she was bucking, and coming. He gave her no time to recover before he plunged his cock deep into her and fucked her mercilessly until she was crying with ecstasy, arching her back and pleading with him to never, never stop.

ARTEMIS SASSE DROVE into the city to do some early Christmas shopping. Her partner, Glen, had called her to say he would be late home and Artemis was enjoying the time alone. She and Glen had not been getting along too well lately, and she knew in her heart that it was over. Still, the thought depressed her. She and Glen had been together since high school, nearly twenty years, and the thought that they would not be in each other's lives much longer was a deep sadness within her. It turned out that it was true, the whole thing about people outgrowing one another. He'd grown one way and she'd grown the other. There was no longer any chance of them meeting in the middle, though they'd tried for a long time.

At thirty-six, Arti had worked her way up in the otherwise male-dominated faculty and was now a tenured professor at the university. There was something missing though, something that wasn't satisfying her in her life, but she couldn't figure out what. She loved her family—she was close to both her sisters and her mother—she had great friends, and ye t...

Something had been bugging at her for a few weeks now, and she couldn't quite reconcile it with her stoic and practical nature. It was Romy, she realized. She felt her middle sister was heading towards trouble and she couldn't figure out why she felt like that. Certainly, Romy was fitting in well at the hospital, or so she said, and she was happy in her small apartment, but Artemis couldn't help feeling scared for her sister.

Why, though? she asked herself again as she browsed around the department store. *Why do I feel like that?*

Maybe it was Dacre, Romy's ex. He was still out there, still angry with Romy for leaving him. The way he had beaten her the last time still haunted Artemis. The hospital in New York had called her and she had flown with her mother and Juno to see Romy. Walking into that room, seeing her sister almost unrecognizable, her face bloodied and bruised, eyes swollen, her leg smashed ... Romy, thankfully, had pressed charges, but Dacre, thanks to his wealthy parents, had hired the best lawyers money could buy and the Sasse women couldn't compete. Dacre had been fined and gave an outward expression of regret, but Romy and her family knew he was enraged by the court case and by the subsequent divorce.

Artemis shook herself. *Romy is an adult and doesn't need you worrying about her. Get a grip.* Artemis asked herself whether she was distracting herself from her failing relationship by focusing so much attention on her sister. She pushed everything to the back of her mind and went to her favorite coffee shop.

A gingerbread latte and a pastry later and she felt the tension leave her body. She was flicking through a book she'd purchased for Juno for Christmas when she felt a hand on her shoulder. Looking up to see a very tall, handsome man, she smiled delightedly. "*Dan?* Dan Helmond?"

Her old friend grinned back at her. "The very one. Hey, kiddo."

Artemis stood and hugged him. Dan had been a couple of years old than she and Glen at school. Now he was a big bear of a man, his dark hair shot through with silver, his beard full. Plaid shirt and camo pants and ear piercings, and Dan looked more like a Hell's Angel than the architect he was. He'd always been a kind, gentle man though, and all the Sasse sisters had had a crush on him at one point or another.

"Can I get you a coffee?" Artemis asked hopefully.

"Nah, I just ordered. Can I get you a top up ... *ugh*, woman, what is that monstrosity?" He peered into her half-empty mug and Artemis grinned.

"It's a gingerbread latte, you philistine, and no, thanks. One sugary hit is enough for me."

Dan excused himself to pay for his own coffee—Americano, no sugar, no cream—and sat down with her. His brown eyes twinkled merrily at her. "Well, now, girl. You're looking good. How's life?"

"It's good, thanks. I'm tenured at my college, family's good. My mom's getting married soon."

Dan looked surprised. "Wow, really? Someone's tamed Magda Sasse?" He always deliberately pronounced their surname 'Sassy' rather than 'Sass,' Artemis remembered.

"I wouldn't say tamed, exactly; you know Mom. She's still a head-in-the-clouds nutso, but wonderful with it." Artemis sipped her coffee. "She's marrying Stuart Eames."

With satisfaction, she saw the amazement on Dan's face. "No freakin' *way*."

"Yes, way."

Dan let out a long breath. "Wow. *Wow*."

"One of his sons is in property ... Gaius Eames. You know him?"

Dan shook his head. "Heard of him, and that star doctor brother of his, but I don't know either. How about you? Still with Glen?"

Barely. "Yes, we're still, um, still ... together."

"You don't seem so sure."

Artemis shrugged, not wanting to talk about Glen with Dan and ruin the atmosphere. "How about you?"

"Wife passed a few years back, cancer." Dan stirred his coffee, clearly lost in those memories for a long moment, such that Arti reached over and touched his hand.

"I'm sorry, Dan."

He nodded and looked up, briefly covering her hand with his and then going on as if he hadn't missed a beat. "I have a seventeen-year-old daughter, Octavia. She's heading off to Harvard next year."

"That's exciting."

Dan beamed and Artemis felt her stomach flutter. *That smile ...* "She's my angel." Dan went on, digging out his wallet and showing her a photograph of a pretty teenager with long dark hair and big soulful brown eyes like her father.

"She's gorgeous. She could be Romy's twin."

"She could. How is your sister doing? Last I heard, she was in New York."

Artemis felt her chest tighten. "She's back now, working as a resident at Rainier Hope. Surgical superstar in the making, so they say."

"I'm not surprised. And Juno?"

"About to work for a charitable foundation in New Orleans."

"Man, the Sasse sisters done good."

Artemis smiled. "We're doing okay."

Dan glanced at his watch. "Listen, Missy, I hate to cut and run but I have a meeting in town —don't suppose you'd like to make this a regular thing? Meeting up for coffee? Tavia's always telling me to slow down, take some time to chill, and I'd like to see you again."

"I'd love to ... here." She pulled a business card out of her pocket, a little worse for wear. "It has my cell phone number on it. Call anytime. It was really great to see you."

Dan bent down and kissed her cheek. "Soon, yeah?"

"Soon."

ARTEMIS FELT ABSURDLY CHEERED as she walked back to her car. *A new friend,* she thought to herself, *a new friend that's an old friend.* She pushed away any thoughts of anything beyond friendship, although she kept rerunning Dan calling her 'Missy'—she'd forgotten that was his name for her back in high school.

When she got home, Glen was in a cheerful mood, and they enjoyed a pleasant meal together for the first time in a long time.

When Glen had gone to bed in his own room, where he'd moved a long time back, Artemis checked her phone to see Dan had already sent her a text message, a photograph of him and his daughter giving her the thumbs up. Sweet and funny.

She went to bed with a huge smile on her face.

From another coffee house across the street, Dacre Mortimer had watched his ex-wife's sister chatting with the tall man. He knew Artemis wouldn't hesitate to call the cops on him if she saw him, and he couldn't risk being caught, not while Romy was still out there in the world, alive. He didn't much care what happened to him after she was dead, but for now, he had a job to do.

Find Romy. Find his beautiful, sexy, love-of-his-life, ex-wife Romy.

And kill her.

6

CHAPTER 6

"Dr. Allende, can I see you about a consult, please?"

Romy hid her grin as Blue looked up from his paperwork and his eyes twinkled at her. "Of course, Dr. Sasse. Where to?"

In less than a minute, they had locked themselves into a supply closet on the quietest floor in the hospital. Blue's lips were against hers, his hands hitching up her skirt as she freed his cock from his pants. He lifted her easily, his strong arms supporting her as she guided his cock inside her. They fucked hard but silently, their eyes locked on the others, their mouths hungrily seeking the other's.

"God, you're amazing." Romy moaned, burying her face in his shoulder to muffle her cry of release.

Blue groaned as he came, panting for air, kissing her so furiously he tasted blood. "You think everyone knows about us?"

"I've been careful ... but we really *should* stop doing this ... God, Blue, that is *not* what I meant by stop, you lunatic."

He was stroking her clit now, relentless until she shivered through another orgasm. "I'm addicted to watching you come," he murmured, his lips against hers, "Your skin flushes such a beautiful color when

I'm fucking you. My cock in your cunt is all I think about all day, all night, and the way you squeeze my dick when I'm inside you."

"God, *Blue!*" Romy's head rolled back as she came again, his dirty talk making her wet and shivery and weak. Blue, grinning, triumphant, thrust his rampant cock back into her and Romy almost screamed with pleasure.

Finally, as they caught their breath, Romy, laughed and shook her head at him. "You are a machine, Allende."

"Love machine." He gave her the finger pistols and she chuckled.

"And you are so cheesy, so, so cheesy."

He kissed her, then helped her straighten her clothes. "Listen, I was thinking ... we should talk about birth control."

"*How to Kill a Mood in Ten Seconds* by Dr. Blue Allende." But she grinned at him. "What are you thinking?"

"We're both doctors, and we both have access to, um, tests. You're right, this isn't sexy, but what I'm leading to is, hopefully."

"And what's that?"

"I want to feel you. Really feel you when I'm inside you. I want to know that when we're doing rounds, you're carrying my seed around with you. Does that sound selfish? I don't mean it to, I just ... I want to be close to you. Oh, damn, I sound like a creep. I'm not explaining this well."

Romy shook her head. "No, but I understand what you're trying to get at. And I want that too." She leaned into him and nuzzled his nose with hers. "Skin on skin," she said in a low, chocolatey voice, "you and me, together." She slid her hand onto his groin, feeling him hardening again.

"Damn, woman, how come I couldn't put it like that?"

Romy chuckled. "Dr. Allende?"

"Yes?"

"When we get back to your apartment tonight, I'm going to suck you dry."

With that, Romy grinned, picked up her files, and headed for the door. "By the way," she said to Blue, who was waiting until his hard-on dissipated, "I had a full work-up last year in New York. I'm clean as a whistle, so to speak. Your move, Doc."

She blew him a kiss and left him in the closet.

ROMY WAS STILL GRINNING when she was called to the emergency room forty-five minutes later. A nervous young intern came to find her. "Hi, Dr. Sasse, I'm sorry to call you personally but there's a patient asking for you. He's in curtain six."

"Name?"

"He won't give me it."

Romy's heart began to thump unpleasantly. *Surely, not.* Surely Dacre hadn't found her already? She smoothed her face out and nodded at the intern. "No problem, I'll see him."

For one awful moment before she pulled back the curtain, she imagined it was her violent ex-husband, that he would lunge for, get his hands around her throat, choke the life out of her.

The relief when she saw the patient was immense, and she smiled at the man, who was cradling a bloody hand. He smiled at her. "Dr. Sasse?"

"That's me, Mr. ...?"

The man grinned, his handsome face lighting up, his blue eyes intense. "Eames. Hey, Romy, I'm Gaius, your soon-to-be stepbrother."

Her eyebrows shot up as she searched for a resemblance to Blue and definitely saw it, now that she was looking for it. The high cheeks and sculpted jaw were apparently genetic. "Hey, well, hey," she stammered and then laughed. "Wow, you caught me off guard. Nice to meet you at last, even if unexpectedly."

Gaius held his hand up. "I was careless while fixing my car."

"Let's take a look."

Romy pulled up a chair and took his hand. "You didn't want to see Dr. Allende?"

"I wanted to meet you. Something good to come out of this. Ouch."

"Sorry." Romy examined the nasty gash. "Well, it's deep, but you won't need surgery. I'll clean it and give you some local anesthetic. Then we can stitch the wound, or even glue it."

Gaius nodded, his eyes never leaving her face. "Thank you, Romy."

As she worked, he asked her questions about her work. "Do you work closely with Blue?"

Was there an edge to his voice? She kept her tone neutral. "Well, he is our General Surgery attending, and that's my chosen specialty. It's strange to think he'll be my brother soon."

"I bet. I didn't think to ask Dad ... have they settled on a wedding date?"

"I don't think so, but Mom's being really secretive about it. Lord knows why; she's not usually shy about anything. Of course, your father's divorce isn't quite final yet, so there's that to consider."

Gaius laughed. "Secrets are overrated. Do you have any secrets, Dr. Sasse?" His voice dropped lower, quieter, and Romy flushed, not out of pleasure, but awkwardness.

He was *flirting* with her, and it was freaking her out. For a second, she imagined saying *Well, your half-brother just reamed me real good in a supply closet, but apart from that ...* "Nope. Boring, I know, but that's me. We're all done here." She gave him a smile and pushed away from him. "The nurse will come to stitch you up."

He reached out and took her arm. "Romy ... thank you. To say thank you, I'd love to take you to dinner. What do you say?"

Romy stepped gracefully away from his grip. "Well, we'll see you at Thanksgiving in a couple of days, and I'm afraid I'm pretty much working until then."

Gaius reached for her hand and kissed the back of it. Instead of the heat that flared through her when Blue touched her, Romy felt her skin go weirdly cold. "Then I shall have to be satisfied with that."

AFTER HE LEFT, Romy felt unsettled. Gaius was all charm and politeness, but there was something underneath the façade, something that made her feel uneasy. She wondered if she should tell Blue that his brother had been in, but eventually decided not to. It was nothing, after all.

She didn't regret her decision that night when Blue dropped a sheet of paper in her lap as he was pulling off his tie. Blood tests. She scanned them and grinned up at him. "Dude, some of these tests take weeks. How did you manage this?"

"Well, honey, let me just say there's a very happy guy in testing right now."

Romy giggled at the mischievous look on Blue's face. "Blue Allende, did you pimp yourself out for tests?"

"Kinda, but not in the way you mean. He might have needed half a week off for a family destination wedding and I might've pulled some big strings."

"Allende, bribery?" she teased. "That's all kinds of wrong."

"I know. I'm disgusted with myself," Blue was grinning widely as he pulled her jeans off of her and knelt between her legs. Romy watched him lazily as he slid her panties down her legs.

Romy hooked her legs over his shoulders. "Lick my pussy, doctor, or I'll forget my promise to milk you dry."

Blue, grinning, buried his face in her sex and Romy closed her eyes, moaning softly as his tongue lashed around her clit, then delved deep into her cunt. He made her come, then she made good on her promise, taking his cock into her mouth and sucking and drawing on him until he came, swallowing down his seed.

Blue scooped her into his arms and carried her to bed, tugging off her sweater and his own, feeling her full breasts soft against his hard chest. He lay on top of her, gazing down at her, stroking the hair back from her face. "So ... do we need to use a condom today?"

Romy shook her head. "I'm on birth control ... let's go for it. I want to feel you inside me."

Blue crushed his lips to hers before slowly burying his cock deep inside her. Romy shivered and Blue groaned. "God, you feel good. Your cunt is so velvety, baby."

They began to move together, Romy savoring every sensation that he sent through her body. A deeper connection was being forged and they gazed at each other, murmuring sweet words to each other as they made love. Romy tilted her hips up so he could go deeper, harder, digging her nails into his buttocks, urging him on. God, this man ... his cock, so big, so thick, reaming her into submission, his intense green eyes soft with love, with desire, with fire, for her ... Romy couldn't quite believe it.

She cried out his name as she came, shuddering and trembling, then felt his seed explode out of him, filling her belly. This man, this incredible man ... she wanted to scream at the top of her voice that she was falling in love with him, that he was her destiny, her dearest desire.

But Romy settled for his sweet kisses, not wanting to spoil the moment with too-soon declarations. But she knew it was true; she was falling for him. Not just his handsome face, his glorious body, or the way he fucked her, both animal-like and yet so tender. It was his sense of humor, his utter lack of ego when he could rightfully claim to be one of the best, his playfulness.

More than anything, Romy felt she could trust him, and after what Dacre had done to her ... it was a big thing for her.

She did tell him that she felt she could trust him (leaving out the parts about Dacre) and to her surprise, Blue looked utterly moved. "I'm glad, *piccolo*. I'm honored by that, and you should know ... I feel the same. Whatever this is between us, whatever it becomes ... you are my person. My lover, my muse, my best friend ... and my family."

Romy's eyes filled with tears. "And you, mine."

Blue kissed her tenderly. "Thank God you came home to Seattle, Romy. Thank God."

And they began to make love again, loving each other long into the night.

GAIUS SMILED GRIMLY to himself as he sat in his car outside his half-brother's apartment. He had followed Romy from the hospital and could hardly believe it when she drove here. He saw Blue come down to greet her, saw them kissing. So his bastard half-brother was fucking his almost- stepsister. Gaius' gut churned with jealousy. Romy Sasse was beautiful, sweet, and of *course*, Blue had gotten there first.

Damn you.

Still, it would make for extra sport, Gaius grinned to himself. Romy Sasse had a whole lot of secrets that he would bet his life Blue didn't know about. The abusive ex-husband, for one.

Dacre Mortimer. Son of New York socialites, a billionaire in his own right. So, Romy liked the money ... that would be useful, although Gaius could see from the divorce papers that she had not asked for a penny from Mortimer, not even the prenup money she had been entitled to. That was interesting.

Gaius also knew Romy had been hospitalized a year previously as she was about to enter her last year of her residency program at Johns Hopkins. Smashed left femur, multiple wounds from a beating, bruised liver, and a burst ovary from being kicked in the stomach. Mortimer's parents had done a good job hushing it up in the papers, but their son had gone to town on Romy when she'd asked for a divorce.

Why the hell had she married him? Gaius couldn't figure it out but if he could find Mortimer, he would ask him. Romy had fled New York as soon as she was well enough and applied to Rainier Hope to finish her residency. A new life.

Hmm. Gaius began to see a whole campaign of terror he could unleash on the couple—especially if he could find Dacre Mortimer and lead him to his ex-wife. He smiled when he thought of watching Dacre confronting his ex-wife, of Blue finding out what had happened. Blue would defend Romy, of course, and maybe Dacre would get rid of Blue, once and for all.

Gaius got excited now. *Yes, yes, this was perfect.* If he could manipulate Mortimer into killing Blue, then he, Gaius, could sweep in and 'save' the day. Poor Romy would be devastated —unless of course, she too was dead. Gaius shrugged. Either way, he would win.

He picked up the phone and called his detective, thanking him for finding out all the information he had already collected, then paused. "I'd like you to do something else for me, and I'm willing to pay you double if you can do it."

"I'm intrigued. Go ahead."

Gaius smiled. "Find out where Dacre Mortimer is, and ask him to meet with you. I have a very interesting proposition for him."

CHAPTER 7

O n Thanksgiving morning, Magda took one look at her fiancé's somber face and sighed. "Uh-oh. What did she do now?"

It had almost become a joke between them; Hilary Eames' attempts to draw out her divorce from Stuart were creative, Magda had to give her that. But Stuart was being worn down by it, his usually merry green eyes losing their sparkle. Magda stood on her tiptoes to kiss him; she was a tall woman herself, but Stuart was a big man, broad-shouldered and long-limbed.

He wrapped his arms around her now. "I can't make head or tail of it, Mags. She's dropping her objections to the divorce."

For a moment, Magda was so shocked, she couldn't speak. After months and months of vicious back-and-forth between Hilary and Stuart, Hilary was dropping her claim for seventy-five percent of Stuart's wealth? How? And more importantly, why? Magda had only met Hilary on two occasions, but it was enough to get a measure of the woman. She liked power, and she loved money. Hilary Eames would not drop her claim to Stuart's billions.

"What the hell?" Magda studied Stuart, who looked lost.

"I just don't know... but I don't trust it."

Magda shook her head. "No. Did you call Gaius, ask him if he knew anything?"

"I did, and he doesn't. He's as bemused as I am. He said he would call her and report back later at dinner."

Magda blew out her cheeks. "So ... she's signing the divorce papers?"

Stuart smiled now. "She is ... which means, my beautiful Magda, we can get married. And soon. I was thinking ... Christmas?"

"It'll be finalized that soon?"

Stuart gave a wry grin. "Sometimes, being rich helps."

"Moneybags." But she kissed him, laughing softly. "I love you, Stuart. If you didn't have a penny, I would still love you to the moon and back."

"Mushy." But he kissed her tenderly, tangling his fingers in her short, steel gray hair. "God, woman, you are beautiful."

She smiled up at him. "Well, you're old. Your eyesight is fading and ... ouch, ouch, no, stop that," she shrieked as he tickled her.

Juno wandered in, hopping up onto the counter and watched them. "Is this some kind of Cocoon foreplay?"

Magda shot her youngest daughter a withering look. "We're not that old. Maybe I don't mind so much that you're moving out after all ..."

Juno smirked and blew her mom a kiss. "You looooove me ..."

Stuart laughed at their antics. "Hey, kiddo," he said to Juno, "I'm trying to persuade your mother to marry me at Christmas. Help me out, would you?"

Juno's eyes went wide. "Vampira's signed the divorce papers?"

"Yup."

Juno did a seated dance of victory, hands raised high in the air. "Yeah, baby! Then, hell yes, Ma, snag this dude before I steal him away from you. Can I officiate?"

Magda and Stuart looked at each other. "Can you get ordained before Christmas?"

Juno looked smug. "Already am. I was waiting for you to

announce your wedding day then I was going to surprise you. What do you say?"

"I say I forgive you for the Cocoon crap," Magda beamed, hugging her youngest tightly. "Stuart ... yes? No?"

Stuart grinned. "I think that would make the day even more perfect, yes. Now all we have to discuss is where."

Magda laughed. "Okay, you two, slow your roll. Let's get today over and done with. Juno, are your sisters on their way?"

"Arti is, but Romy said she might be a little late. Emergency at the hospital, and she said that she and Blue might come together for convenience's sake."

"That's cool ... but I hope they don't get tied up."

ROMY WAS INDEED TIED up but not in the way her mother meant. Blue's tie was wrapped around her wrists, her hands behind her back as she lay on his dining table, her legs wrapped around his waist as he plunged his cock in and out of her, thrusting harder each time as he fucked her, his strokes brutal but his hands on her body, caressing her breasts, her belly, were soft and tender. Romy came explosively as Blue pulled out and came on her skin, shooting thick reams of creamy white come onto her belly.

Romy begged him not to stop, and so he turned her onto her stomach, pulling her hands, and she cried out with pain and pleasure. He pushed into her perfectly rounded ass and fucked her slowly this time. "God, Romy, you're so beautiful, so exquisite ... I'll never get enough of you, not ever..."

He made her come over and over before, exhausted, they showered together then fell onto his bed. They had been working an all-nighter and had gotten home just after dawn. After sleeping for an hour, they both woke, horny for each other and for the next three hours, fucked each other's brains out, clawing at each other, desperate for that connection.

Now they lay side by side, sleepy and exhausted. Blue grabbed the alarm clock and set an alarm for two p.m. "Don't want to be late for your mom." He grinned, but then saw Romy had fallen asleep, her head resting in the crook of his shoulder. Blue studied her face, so lovely, so expressive even in repose. He knew he was in love with her, had been for weeks now, almost since the first, but Blue struggled with whether to tell her or not. They needed to get this dinner with their parents over with, then decide whether or not to go public.

The only person Blue had told was his chief of surgery, Beau Quinto, not wanting any improper behavior on his record, nor to let his mentor and friend down.

"It isn't a fling, Beau," he'd told him seriously, "I'm crazy about her, but it won't affect either my work or Romy's. We're professionals. Yes, Romy and I work closely together, but I assure you I don't favor her above the other residents." He grinned slightly. "Even if she is the best general surgery resident I've ever seen."

Quinto had rolled his eyes. "Blue ... I've been where you are. When I met Dinah, she was a patient, so I know all about improper relationships. I trust you and Romy not to let your relationship interfere with your work. Don't let me down."

"I won't, I give you my word. Thanks, boss."

Blue laid his head on top of Romy's and closed his eyes. Feeling her in his arms was like a drug to him; he loved her brain, her commitment to her work, to the hospital ... God, he'd dreamed of finding a woman like Romy all his adult life. The only person who had ever gotten close was Julia, his college sweetheart, but she had had an affair with Gaius during their final year at Harvard. When a vindictive Gaius had dumped her soon after, Blue had had no interest in resuming the relationship though he hadn't wished his brother's cruelty on her. He wouldn't wish it on anybody.

Gaius had always been resentful of Blue, of anything he had that Gaius didn't. Success, focus, commitment —Gaius thought these things were something one either had or didn't have, rather than things one would work for. Blue had no time for his feckless older half-sibling, and even less time for his stepmother. Hilary had made Blue's mother's life a misery while she was alive, and continued to besmirch her memory after death.

He shook himself now. Later, he would have to see Gaius and not give away that he was in love with Romy. He had nightmares about Gaius setting his malevolent sights on the beautiful young woman in his arms. Of course, they were nothing to the other nightmares that had plagued him ever since the eight young women were brutalized in the city, since Yasmin Levant had died on his operating table. She *had* looked like Romy, too much for Blue not to imagine it was his love bled out and dead in the O.R.

His arms tightened reflexively around her now and he pressed his lips to her forehead. Romy murmured in her sleep and opened her eyes, smiling up at him. He kissed her soft lips, treasuring every moment, before she sighed and went back to sleep.

God, I love you, piccolo. He hadn't exaggerated when he'd told her he wanted to whisk her away to Italy, to show her every place he'd loved as a child, everywhere he had been at his happiest until he'd met her.

He closed his eyes and slept then, with that happy dream in mind, until the alarm went off at two p.m., and he and Romy made love again before finally dragging themselves from their beds to go celebrate Thanksgiving with their blended family.

HE HAD BEEN FOLLOWING Artemis for weeks now, and finally, she had led him to the Sasse family home. When he and Romy had been married, she had been cagey about where her mother lived, scared of him even on their wedding night. Dacre smiled to himself, remembering. She hadn't wanted to sleep with him, and as she'd held out until they were married, Dacre had been certain of one thing. He would fuck Romy on their wedding night if it killed him ... or her. It had taken his forearm across her throat before she gave in, tears pouring down her face as he forced her legs apart.

"You are *mine*," he growled at her continually. He'd worn her down over the months to be able to get her to agree to marry him, destroying her confidence, isolating her from her friends.

By the time of the wedding—fifteen minutes at City Hall—Romy had been a shadow of her former self. Dacre still wasn't certain how he'd scared her so much that she'd actually agreed to be legally bound to him, but such was his power, he now remembered proudly. That, and keeping her away from her damn nosy family so they couldn't run interference.

She'd spoken her vows in such a quiet voice the judge had had to ask her to speak up twice, but when she had seen the barely concealed rage on Dacre's face, she had quailed and recited them louder, but in a monotone. Dacre had seen the two witnesses, strangers he had wrangled from a bar, exchange concerned looks. The woman with them had slipped Romy her number. *If you need anything.* He knew Romy hadn't called her. It would have made no difference if she had.

Dacre killed the woman, Regan, a few weeks later, catching her unawares as she stepped out into a dark alley in the back of the bar where she worked to have a smoke. Hand across her throat, knife in her belly, one, two, three.

Dead. God, the feeling, the rush it gave him, and every single time he imagined his victim was Romy. His cock would harden and he would smell the blood, imagining it to be hers. That sweet gasp of shock and pain as the knife sliced through flesh was Romy's ... she never made any noise when they had sex, would never kiss him on the mouth. She didn't fake orgasm and it made him crazy. When he'd found out she was back in touch with her family that had been the last straw and when the beatings had started.

That last one, the final one, had begun when she was late home from the hospital and he'd been drinking. Such a normal thing, but he'd heard her coming up the stairs and for a moment, he had just been joking around, hiding behind the door to spook her.

He had hooked his arm around her neck and she had screamed in fright. Pulling away from him, she'd rounded on him with wide, frightened eyes, so beautiful in her terror, and told him she was leaving him for good. Dacre had lost it. He'd beat her mercilessly until she could no longer stand, blood pouring from cuts above her eyes, her nose broken, her mouth bleeding. He'd pulled her hair until she sobbed, then, as she slumped to the floor, he had stamped on her left thigh and they'd both heard the decisive crack as her femur shattered. Romy, choking on her own blood, could no longer scream for help.

Dacre had studied her dispassionately, then, grabbing a knife from the block, had raped his broken wife. He had intended to kill her, he knew that now, but when he'd heard his neighbors shouting, banging on the door, he'd chickened out. Instead, he'd called an ambulance for Romy, turning on the waterworks, apologizing over and over, begging her to live.

At the hospital, the police had arrested him and he'd made a great show of not protesting. Secretly he had been waiting for his lawyer to tell him Romy was dead, that her injuries were too bad. The police had discovered who he was and their whole attitude had changed. His father had friends high up in the NYPD. He had been cautioned and told that if Romy pressed charges, they would have to revisit.

His mother and father had been beside themselves with grief. They had adored Romy and had thought she would be able to tame some of Dacre's excesses. When it became clear Romy would live and that she would be throwing the book at him, Dacre's father, Hubert, had paid off the people he needed to drop the charges in return for a plea deal. No jail time for Dacre. Romy and her family had fought back, but they were no match.

In return, Romy had been given her divorce but would not take a penny from the Mortimers. Hubert Mortimer had given his son a check for three million dollars and then cut him off. His parents had disowned him entirely.

And you are to blame, Romy Sasse. You shouldn't have made me angry.

Dacre parked his car behind the tree line of the forest which bordered Magda Sasse's property and stepped out to slink closer to the house. He saw a car pull up and saw a dark haired-man and Romy get out. They were laughing and joking. God, Romy looked so beautiful. Dacre's cock twitched at the sight of her long dark hair tumbling around her lovely face. Who was this guy with her?

The next moment, he watched as the man pulled Romy into a

small corner of the house, shaded from the windows, and kissed her. Romy gazed up at the man with love in her eyes and it made Dacre's insides twist in rage.

Damn fucking bitch. How dare she cheat? Because she was still his in spite of the divorce. She'd vowed forever and she would always be, no matter her whoring ways.

"She's exquisite, isn't she?"

Dacre started and turned to find a tall, amused-looking man with piercing blue eyes staring at him. Dacre was lost for words. The man held his hand out.

"You must be Dacre Mortimer," he said in a friendly tone. He nodded towards the couple who were now disappearing into the house. "And that's my bastard half-brother Blue Allende kissing your ex-wife. And yes, they're fucking each other. Sickening, isn't it?"

"And who the fuck are you?"

"Gaius Eames. Hello, Mortimer. I think we're going to have a lot of fun together."

CHAPTER 8

Romy was beginning to feel really uncomfortable. The meal had started off well. Everyone had been formally introduced, and the food was out of this world. If there was one thing Magda excelled at apart from parenting and sculpting, it was cooking. The turkey was juicy and plentiful, the side dishes of creamy mashed potatoes and yams sweet and heavenly, the gravy well-seasoned. Even the cranberry sauce was made from scratch and Blue grinned at her as she went in for another helping.

She shrugged unrepentantly. "It's my favorite."

The worst part of the meal was not giving away that she and Blue were together, not sharing those intimate glances or private jokes between them. They'd slipped a couple of times but had written it off as 'work jokes.'

Everything had been going really well until Gaius turned his attention to her.

"Nice to see you again so soon, Romy."

Oh, fuck. "How's the hand?" She could feel Blue staring at her curiously.

"Much, much better, thanks to you." Gaius appeared friendly, even if there was an undercurrent. He looked at Blue. "She's quite remarkable, Blue. Have you noticed?"

"Of course," Blue smiled smoothly, but the edge in the smile was one Romy hadn't seen before and it made her cold. "Romy is by far the best resident at Rainier Hope this year. And for many years, come to that."

"You sound impressed, brother."

Blue fixed Gaius with a searching stare. "I am, Gaius. When did you and Romy meet?"

Romy opened her mouth to speak but Gaius got there first. "A couple of days ago ... you didn't mention it, Romy?" His face was a picture of innocent confusion.

"Patient privacy," Romy said quietly. She risked a glance at Blue, who met her gaze steadily. *There will be questions later*, his eyes said, and she gave a quick, almost imperceptible nod, believing with every fiber of her being that he might be upset but would not hurt her as Dacre had done anytime he was enraged.

"The consummate professional," Gaius said.

Artemis cleared her throat, picking up on the sudden tension. "I actually have some news."

Romy shot her a grateful smile. "Is everything okay?"

"Oh, yes ... well, no, but yes, and I know that doesn't make sense. Glen and I have decided to break up. Now I know you'll think this is a bad thing, Mom, but for both Glen and I ... we've grown apart. Neither of us thinks badly of the other, it's just we no longer fit as a couple. Glen's moving out ... today, actually, which is why he couldn't be here. It's entirely amicable, I assure you, so there's no need to pick sides, etc."

"I'm glad," Juno said immediately, "but you know we've always got your back, Arti."

Artemis grinned at her.

"I know you do, Bubba. But, yeah, so ... I guess I'm just saying, I'm single, and happily so for now."

"As long as you're happy, darling," Magda looked a little upset, but smiled at her eldest daughter, always supportive. Artemis leaned over and squeezed her hand.

"I am, Mom, and so is Greg. So, can anybody cheer proceedings up? Mom, Stuart?" She grinned at them. "I hear someone very special is going to marry the two of you?"

Juno beamed as Romy and Blue looked surprised. "Really, Juno? That's awesome. Hey," Romy said in a stage-whisper to her sister, "When they get to the kissing bit, can you leave that out? I don't want to see that."

Magda threw a brussels sprout at her daughter. "Cheeky girl."

THE REST of the meal passed in easy conversation and laughter, but Romy could feel the tension rolling off Blue's body. It didn't help that Gaius, pretending there was a friendship between he and Romy, made jokes with her, flattering her as if they had known each other for more than a few moments. Romy saw her sisters looked confused at the strange behavior and when they got her on her own, clearing the dishes, they questioned her about it. Romy shrugged.

"I don't get it either. I treated him for his hand wound, that was it. I don't know the man. Perhaps he's just trying to, I don't know, ingratiate himself."

"Then why isn't he all pally-pally with me and Arti?" Juno shook her head. "Guy's a creep."

"For God's sake, Juno, lower your voice." Artemis hissed at her and Juno rolled her eyes. Romy felt a lump of misery settle in her chest. She should have told Blue; that he was pissed was obvious—to her, at least. *Damn it.* She looked at Artemis and for a moment debated telling her about how she felt about Blue. No, it wasn't fair to him; they had vowed to keep it quiet, at least until after Stuart and Magda's wedding. She turned back to the dishes, only half-listening, as her sisters chatted.

Eventually she was alone in the kitchen, making work for herself. She felt a hand on the back of her neck and turned hopefully, expecting to see Blue. She jerked backwards when she saw it was Gaius instead. He held up his hands.

"Sorry, I didn't mean to startle to you, Romy; it just seemed like you were tensed up there."

Romy was trembling. "Gaius, please don't touch me unless I ask you to."

"Sorry." His smile was innocent, but his eyes sparkled with malice. "Guess you're always a little jumpy these days. After what your husband did to you in New York."

Romy was so shocked that she didn't see Blue enter the kitchen behind her as Gaius started to grin. It was only when she heard him put down the casserole dish he was carrying that she turned—and saw the hurt in his eyes. He gazed back at her for a beat then turned and walked out. Romy stared after him in dismay.

"Was it something I said?" Gaius asked, and laughed coldly.

CHAPTER 9

Blue was silent as he drove Romy back to her apartment. Romy sat in miserable contemplation as he followed her into her small apartment and shut the door. In spite of her total trust in him, her nerves were tightly wound, fear unavoidable. She waited for the storm as they walked into the living room, but he just grabbed a bottle of scotch from her kitchen with two glasses and sat her down next to him.

"Now," he said quietly, calm and patient, the utter antithesis of Dacre, "tell me everything."

Romy took a deep breath in, pressing her hands tightly together. "It's true, I was married, although I don't know how the hell Gaius knew. Incidentally, he's an asshole for behaving as if he and I were better acquainted than a five-minute consult the other night."

Blue nodded slowly. "But you didn't tell me about it."

"No, and right now, I don't know why. Blue, he's a creep, and he came onto me then as well as tonight. He makes my skin crawl."

Blue looked slightly mollified. "That's Gaius, all right. But why didn't you tell me you were married?"

"We weren't—aren't—there yet. You've never told me about your past lovers either."

"Don't do that, Romy. No games. Husband is a lot different from girlfriend. Who was he?"

Romy looked at him steadily. "He was a violent, ignorant spoiled rich boy who tried to kill me. There. Now you know."

"What?" Blue said in obvious horror.

Romy was glad he was shocked. "That's why I didn't tell you. I don't like to talk about it, frankly. It's a lot more complicated than just 'I was married.' He regularly beat me and raped me, then when I told him I wanted a divorce, he assaulted me so violently that I nearly died. He comes from a rich family. He's arrogant, entitled ... Dacre Mortimer is a monster and if he finds me, I'm dead. So, the fewer people that know about him, the fewer people there are both in his firing line, and who can help him find me. Why do you think my photo and name aren't on the Rainier Hope website or in promotional material? He knows I live in Seattle, he just doesn't know where." She sighed and rubbed her face. "Obviously, Gaius has done his homework."

"*Jesus*, Romy." Blue got up and paced around. "Why did you marry him in the first place?"

"That's a question I still can't answer fully for myself," she said softly. "He ... cowed me. Separated me from my mother and sisters. I guess after months of nonstop abuse, you get broken down to where a person can make you do just about anything. Even marrying the devil himself."

To Romy's great relief, Blue came back to her and put his arms around her, holding her tightly. He buried his face in her hair and Romy was shocked to feel him shaking.

"Blue?"

"The thought of anything happening to you." His voice was muffled and his arms tightened around her.

"It's okay, baby; nothing's going to happen to me." Romy made him look at her and she stroked his face, wondering how she could ever have wondered even slightly if this man would hurt her. He was such a good man, God. How had she gotten so lucky this time? "I'm sorry I didn't tell you about Gaius. I just didn't want to upset you. That's clearly want he wants, to drive a wedge between us."

Blue pressed his lips to hers. "Romy ... that won't ever happen. I won't let it. I'm in love with you. The thought of anyone hurting you kills me."

It was Romy's turn to cry now. "I love you too, Doc," she smiled through her tears and he kissed her passionately. Romy pressed her body to his. "Take me to bed, Dr. Allende."

He undressed her slowly, kissing each piece of exposed skin until her whole body vibrated with longing. Naked, she wrapped her legs around him and took him in, his cock thrusting deep into her cunt in long, measured strokes. His lips moved with hers, tender and loving as they made love. Blue's eyes were intense on hers.

"Let's tell our family, tell them we're in love. I'm shocked they didn't guess." He began to smile as Romy moaned with pleasure as he buried himself deeper inside. "I want to tell the world about the woman I love, the brilliant, beautiful Romy ... I promise you. I'll keep you safe and loved. So, so loved ..."

Romy cried out his name as she came, her back arching up, her thighs tightening as he came inside her, his lips at her throat. "Yes," she said, as they caught their breath, "Yes, Blue ... yes ..."

In the morning, Romy was changing into her scrubs when Mac came to find her. "You look different," he remarked. "Glowing. You're not knocked up, are you?"

"No, definitely not," she rolled her eyes in amusement. "What's going on today? It's like a ghost town." Virtually none of the regular staff had been present when she'd walked into the hospital.

Mac's smile faded. "You haven't heard? Another massacre. Four women found in the grounds of the Gasworks. All stabbed. They were brought to the ER, but they were all D.O.A. Everyone is cleaning up that mess and/or doing paperwork and/or talking to police. Again. I'm so sick of police."

"Oh God, not again." Romy felt sick. She followed Mac out of the locker room as he headed for rounds.

"And get this," he went on. "None of them knew each other. Police think they were all picked for some reason and then left together. One of them had her femur smashed like Yasmin Levant."

Romy stopped. "What did you say?"

"Left femur smashed. Why?"

A curl of horror was beginning to form inside of her, a doubt, a horrific idea. Murders in New York and now Seattle ... smashed femur ... *no, you're being paranoid and ridiculous, Sasse.* "Can I see the records?"

Mac shrugged. "Sure." They walked down to the ER, Romy assuring Mac she'd smooth things over with Blue if they were late for rounds. Romy picked up the files from the desk and read through them. There were multiple stab wounds, and all of the women were dark haired and dark eyed, with olive skin.

"Huh."

She looked up at Mac, who was studying the files with an odd expression his face. "What?"

"I just noticed. Their names. *Roberta, Ornella, Margaret, Ynez.* Their initials spell your name."

Romy felt like she'd been hit in the chest by a sledgehammer. No, it had to be a coincidence. She turned to the computer and brought up the case files for Yasmin Levant and the other women who had died with her. Reading through the names, she looked at Mac, whose eyes were now troubled. Drawing in a deep breath, Romy logged on the Internet and Googled the murders in New York. "Oh God ..."

All of the victims had names whose initials spelled her first name. Mac put his hand on her shoulder. "You know, Roms, this really could be coincidence—"

"It isn't." Romy began to tremble. "I need to talk to the police."

Mac looked alarmed. "You don't know who it is, do you?"

Romy nodded grimly. "I do. I have to find Blue."

Upstairs, Blue looked up, but his smile faded when he saw her face. He stood up and walked over to her immediately, reaching for her. "What is it, sweetheart?"

Romy drew in a deep breath. "It's Dacre. He's in Seattle. He's coming for me."

CHAPTER 10

A rtemis tried not to feel too excited as she made her way
through the icy streets of Seattle to the coffee house. She
and Dan had met up a few times but this day was the first
time when she was a free agent. Glen had moved out over the week-
end, and although they had both been sad, even cried a little, Artemis
had never felt so convinced they were doing the right thing.

And now she was going to see Dan, the man who had been
haunting her dreams for weeks now. She'd repeatedly told herself it
was just a friendship, but she couldn't mistake the look in Dan's eyes
when he was with her, and she was sure it was reflected in hers.
Desire. A bond. She had never felt so comfortable with a man in her
life, so at ease and relaxed—at the same time, every time she was
with him, all she wanted to do was rip his clothes off and kiss him
until she couldn't breathe.

She felt some guilt—after all, she and Glen had only just split—
but then again, they'd lived separate lives for so many years. It was
time to move on, and today was a big step forward doing just that.
Today Dan was bringing his teenage daughter to meet her. He had
asked Artemis if she wouldn't mind, his face going red, and Artemis
knew she was being assessed for ... something. God, she hoped she

would pass the test, and it wasn't helping her nerves but as soon as she pushed open the door to the coffee house, Dan and his female mini-me both grinned at her and Artemis relaxed.

Octavia was a delightful mix of typical teenager and nerdy geek. She reminded Artemis both of Juno with her confidence and Romy in her dark looks. She told Octavia that and the young woman smiled. "Dad said the same thing. He's always talked about the Sassy Sasse Sisters—you're almost legendary in our house."

"Really?" Artemis was absurdly flattered and Dan rolled his eyes.

"Way to ruin my game, kiddo."

Octavia chuckled. "Sorry, Pa, but it's the truth. I'd love to meet your sisters."

"We can arrange that, though Juno is leaving for New Orleans soon. Romy is still here, though, at the hospital."

They chatted easily for an hour then Octavia got up. She kissed Artemis's cheek. "Sorry I have to cut and run, but I have study group."

Her father coughed something which sounded suspiciously like 'geek.' Octavia grinned. "I am what you made me. Bye, Missy, I hope we see each other again soon. Pa, I'll probably stay over at Gail's tonight, so don't wait up."

"Just text me if you are."

"Will do. Bye." And she was gone.

Artemis grinned at Dan. "She's great."

Dan grinned, delighted. "I know, she's a good kid. I think you have her approval."

"Ha, I hope so." Artemis met his gaze and held it, blushing furiously, but Dan, his dark eyes twinkling, smiled in a way that made her stomach flutter.

"Missy?"

"Yes?" Her heart was beating out of her chest and she felt breathless.

"I'm gonna kiss you now." Dan leaned over and brushed her lips with his, lightly, before the kiss deepened and went on for a long moment. Artemis sank into his embrace, feeling his hands cup her face. "God, Missy, if you knew how long I've wanted to do that."

Artemis smiled. "Me too. What happens now?"

"Well, option A ... we stay here kissing all day. Option B ... I take you back to my place, undress you slowly, and kiss every inch of your perfect skin, before we make love tenderly. Option C ... we throw caution to the wind and fuck each other's brains out. Feel free to mix the last two options." He was grinning, and Artemis started to laugh.

"Dan Helmond, I say ... Option C first, then option B. Option A can go hang."

Before she could finish her sentence, Dan had grabbed her hand and they were running towards his car. In thirty minutes they were naked in his bed, and Dan was thrusting his enormous, thick cock deep inside her as they fucked hard. Artemis threw every caution to the wind; she had an animal desire in her for this man, his huge, muscled body making her feel so small and precious, his kisses both tender and feral.

Afterwards they ordered pizza and ate it in bed, feeling like lovesick teens again. Artemis grinned at Dan's self-satisfied expression. "Don't think for a minute, Helmond, that I left Glen for you."

"Yeah, you did." But she could tell he was joking around, and laughed. "Admit it, woman, you had to have the Dan-Dan-Man."

"Oh, jeez, I'm leaving," she groaned and giggled as he pulled her back into his arms and kissed her. "Marinara kisses."

"Think I got some mozzarella action going on in my beard if you're interested." His smile was so wide, Artemis couldn't help giggling until she cried.

"That's so gross. Your seduction game is poor, Helmond."

"You love it, Missy Sassy."

She kissed him then. "I do. You may be crazy, but I'm crazy about you. If I'm honest, I'm kind of relieving a high-school fantasy right now."

Dan grinned, smoothing her blonde hair back from her face. "Except this is no fantasy. This is real, Missy." His face was serious now, but Artemis could see the love in his eyes. "I'm all in, Missy. You and me, this is all I want."

Artemis sighed happily, leaning into his embrace. "Me too, big guy, me too."

"Stay with me tonight."

She nodded, her lips suddenly too busy to speak, and they made love again, slowly this time, exploring each other's body, forgetting the time, long into the night.

ROMY SIPPED HER NOW-COLD COFFEE. She had been with the police most of the day and now she and Blue sat together in the interview room as the detective in charge of the homicides questioned her again.

"I'm sorry if I'm repeating questions, Dr. Sasse, but it's important. Now, it could be a coincidence, but we always look for patterns and we had noticed the women who died shared the same first name initial. But until you came forward we didn't know who the message was intended for."

Blue groaned in dismay and the detective looked at him. "Don't worry, Dr. Allende. We have a state-wide BOLO out for Dacre Mortimer. If he's here, we'll find him. In the meantime, we'll assign you protection, Dr. Sasse."

"I can handle that." Blue said, his voice gruff. "The best protection money can buy. He won't get near you, Romy."

God, was this really happening? Romy closed her eyes and asked herself if she was really that shocked. Dacre would never have accepted her leaving him ... but to kill all these innocent victims to send her a message? "Why didn't he just kill me?" Her voice was quiet and surprisingly calm.

"Don't." Blue was barely holding onto his composure. The detective smiled at them.

"You've been unbelievably brave and helpful in coming forward. Go home and get some rest. I'll be in touch."

.   .   .

ROMY ASKED Blue to drive her to her mother's house. "I want them all to know what's going on—it's not fair to them not to know that they might in danger too. Dacre is a monster."

Her heart sank, however, when they got to her mother's house. Gaius was there too, meeting with his father.

Magda knew something was wrong, clearly, as she gazed at her middle daughter. "Romy?"

Blue took Romy's hand. "Magda, Dad ... we have something to tell you. Two things. One, we hope you'll be happy about, because we are. Romy and I have been seeing each other for a while now, and Magda, I'm so in love with your daughter ..."

Magda exclaimed in delight and threw her arms around them. "I thought I sensed something!"

Stuart grinned widely, clapping his son on the back. "Son, I'm delighted for you both."

"Oh, Romy ... sweetheart, finally. I'm so happy you found a good man at long last." Magda was in tears, and Romy teared up a little too before adding to the overall level of emotion.

"Mom ...There's something else."

Gaius, smirking in the background, leaned forward, his eyes glittering with spite. "Don't be shy, sis, tell us."

Romy flushed at the jibe, but she felt Blue squeeze her hand. "Shut the fuck up, Gaius; this isn't the time for your malice. Magda, Dad, I'm afraid that it isn't all good news. We think Dacre Mortimer is in Seattle."

"God, no." Magda went pale and clutched at her daughter's hand. "Sit down with us, sweethearts, and tell us what's going on."

As Romy told them about the murders, about the signature that had led her to suspect Dacre was behind them. "I knew, or I should have known, he would come after me. He has nothing to lose by murdering me. His family has already cut him off; revenge is all he has left."

Blue cleared his throat and Romy looked at him. His beautiful eyes were deeply troubled and she could feel the tension in his body. "Dad ... I've already set the ball rolling for added protection. I know it's inconvenient, especially with the wedding coming up, but I won't risk any of us getting hurt." He paused, then glanced at his half-brother. "Gaius, you too. And I think perhaps you'd better clue your mother in, too."

"That's very thoughtful of you." Gaius's voice was a monotone and Romy couldn't tell whether he was being sincere or not. She studied him ... the malice had gone from his eyes and he didn't smile. He looked at her. "As long as you're okay, Romy, that's all *I* care about."

Fucker. That tone was back in his voice, the intimate one, the one that said *I know you better than you know.* His smirk was back too. Romy looked away from him. Blue pressed his lips against her temple.

"*Piccolo*, I know this is fast, but I'd feel a hell of a lot better if you moved in with me."

"I would too, Romy," her mother added quickly, and Romy nodded.

"Fine. Yes, of course. God, I'm sorry about this, everyone."

Magda looked angry now. "Listen here, my girl, you have nothing to be sorry about. It's that ... asshole. He should have gone to jail when he hurt you last year. Bastard. I could kill him with my bare hands. I will if he ever comes in spitting distance of me."

LATER, when Blue and Romy got back to his apartment, Blue made her drink some hot tea, Romy shivering uncontrollably. "I thought it was all over," she said in a low voice, "I was so stupid."

"No." Blue wrapped his arms around her, kissing her gently. "There are crazy people all around. It has nothing to do with any choices you've made in life. I won't let anything happen to you."

Romy leaned into him. "It's weird. I'm scared, but at the same time, I can't recall ever being as happy as I am with you right now. I love you, Blue."

"And I love you, baby. Maybe we should go away for a while."

Romy shook her head. "He'll just kill more people. If he knows I'm here, he can try and get to me and then we'll have him."

"Christ, Romy, you're not bait, here." Blue's voice rose and then fell just as quickly. "Sorry, I didn't mean to snap, but we have to take this seriously. You saw what he did to Yasmin Levant."

"I did see," Romy said quietly. "I watched her die, remember? Right alongside you."

Blue blanched and yanked her hard into his chest. "I'm sorry, baby. Forgive me, *piccolo*. I didn't mean—I just—the thought of you in harm's way makes me insane."

She curled into his warm, hard strength. "I won't deliberately put myself in his sights, but once we confirm it is him ... maybe, just maybe I can help catch him. I need to do *something*, Blue. Those poor girls."

Blue drew in a deep breath. "For tonight, let's just ... try and forget him. This place is secure. Tomorrow I'll call in a security team. Baby, do you feel safe?"

"With you, always." She kissed him and he stroked her face, half-smiling.

"Regardless of the circumstances, I'm glad you're here. I was thinking about asking you to move in this morning, but then the sensible part of me said it might scare you off."

Romy smiled at him. "It might have done this morning, although I loved waking up with you." She sighed. "I hate that the reason I'm here is that bastard."

"No," Blue said, his lips brushing her, "the reason you're here is that we love each other."

"You got that right, Doc." Romy pressed her body against his, and Blue held her tightly.

"Are you tired, *piccolo*?"

Romy smiled. "No ... but I am starving."

Blue laughed. "Of course, forgive me. Well, how about some old fashioned Italian comfort food?"

"Pasta? Sold. Shall we order in?"

Blue pretended to look affronted. "How dare you?"

Romy giggled. "You can cook?"

Blue got up and pulled her to her feet, throwing her over his shoulder and carrying her to his state-of-the-art kitchen. "Can I cook? I'm Italian, *piccolo*. Sit here," he dumped her onto a stool, "and watch the maestro at work."

Romy watched him cook pasta, rolling out the dough and making the ravioli with deft efficiency. He kept up a stream of instructions, just as he did in the operating theater, and when the pasta was cooked, Romy almost swooned at the garlicky, oozy, buttery taste.

"God, Allende," she mumbled over a huge mouthful, "is there anything you're not good at?"

He pretended to consider, then shrugged. "Nope." He laughed as she threw her napkin at him.

"There's one thing you didn't think of, Dr. Wonderpants. I now have garlic breath."

"Ha," he said, "so do I." He pressed his lips against hers and they both decided that it wasn't an issue as the kiss deepened and soon the remnants of the pasta were forgotten as Blue tumbled her to the floor.

FOR THE NEXT FEW HOURS, Blue did his best to make her forget everything else but the blissful release of making love, but as the night wore on and he fell asleep, Romy lay awake.

Just as I find happiness, Dacre comes for me. Bastard.

Now that the fear had dissipated a little, she felt anger at the injustice of it. All those innocent girls. Romy eased out of Blue's arms and got out of bed, walking to the huge picture window that looked out over Seattle. Romy leaned her forehead against the cold glass and stared down at the streets below.

Wherever you are, Dacre, come for me. I'm ready for you, you piece of shit. Come for me.

I'm ready.

CHAPTER 11

*N*ew Orleans

JUNO SASSE SPRAWLED on her friend's couch and watched as Livia balanced a plate of cookies on her huge, pregnant belly. Juno grinned at her. "I can't believe you're having a baby, Livvy. When you think where you were a year ago."

Livia Chatelaine smiled at her friend. "You're not the only one who can't believe it, darling. When Sandor stabbed me, then put that bullet in me, I thought that was it. I was a goner. Still, that's in the past." She smoothed her dress over her bump. "And this little girl is almost here. I cannot wait."

Juno grinned. "My first niece."

"You betcha. Speaking of which, you haven't filled me in on what your sisters are up to. Has Arti married Glen yet? What about Romy? Does she like the hospital in Seattle?"

"So many questions," Juno laughed. "Okay, in order, *no, they broke up; she's fine*; and *yes*."

Livia almost spat out her cookie. "Glen and Arti what?"

"They split," Juno repeated. "It wasn't a nasty breakup or anything, they'd just grown apart."

"Wow. So much for fairy tales," Livia muttered in dismay. "Except mine. I won't deny I'm living the dream. Poor Arti though."

"I think she's much happier, actually," Juno said. "Now, the real gossip is Romy. Talk about fairy tales. She's in love ... with our soon-to-be step-brother Blue. Here ..." She grabbed Livia's iPad and typed something in, then showed Livia the photo of Blue Allende. Livia's eyes opened wide.

"Wow, he's gorgeous ... and he and Romy?"

"Are fucking each other's brains out. They've only just told Mom and Stuart, but I knew a while back."

Livia grinned at Juno's smug expression. "They told you?"

"No, I went for coffee with them unexpectedly, and it was so obvious." Her smile faded. "After what Romy's ex did to her ..."

Livia nodded, her eyes sad. "And they think he's the one behind the murders?"

"Yup. God, the thought of something happening to her again ... she's so tiny, Liv, and she can kick ass, believe me, but Dacre is a sick fuck."

Livia pushed herself from her chair, somewhat awkwardly, and came to hug her friend. "Juno, you can't let it rule your life. I bet Romy is back at work today, saving lives. I remember when Sandor was waging his campaign ... the thought of him hurting Nox or Odelle ... if Romy feels half the anger I did, she won't let Dacre near her or anyone she loves."

Juno felt comforted by her friend's words and when she was in bed later, in the sumptuous guestroom of Nox and Livia's mansion, she called Romy, surprised when her sister picked up straight away.

"Well timed, Juno Boo." Romy sounded cheerful, "I just got out of a four-hour surgery and am on a break. How's NOLA? How are Livvy and gorgeous Nox?"

"New Orleans is warm," Juno teased, hearing Romy's jealous

groan. "Livvy is blooming, about to pop any second, and Nox is, well, delicious as always. You okay, Romulus?"

"I am good," Romy said determinedly. "No fucker is messing with me."

"You got seriously laid last night, didn't you?" Juno laughed as her sister giggled.

"Last night, this morning, and as soon as Blue finishes up, in about five minutes. The on-call room is free."

"Babe, you've turned into a nympho. Seriously, though, are you okay?"

"I really, really am, Boo. Please don't worry."

Juno heard voices in the background and then the familiar voice of Blue. She heard her sister laugh. "I guess you need to, um, get off ... the phone, I mean."

Romy laughed. "You guessed, right. You're okay, though, right?"

"I am. I really am. I'll talk to you tomorrow."

"Okay. I love you."

"Love you too."

Juno clicked off her phone and snuggled down in her bed. Romy sounded happy, and not cowed by what was happening, and Juno had to be happy with that. She fell asleep and was woken three hours later by Livia shouting to Nox that the baby was coming.

SEATTLE

Romy moaned as Blue's cock thrust deeper and deeper inside her, his lips hungry on hers, on her throat, sucking at her nipples as he fucked her. She gripped his dark curls tightly, their lovemaking animal and feral.

"Christ, woman, you drive me crazy," Blue groaned, slamming his hips against hers, sinking balls deep into her ready and swollen cunt. Romy was almost delirious with pleasure and her orgasm hit hard, leaving her breathless and with her head swimming. Blue came, shooting thick, creamy cum deep inside her belly and she clamped her legs around him, keeping him locked inside of her. His dark brown hair was damp with sweat, his skin salty, his eyes sleepy with love and pure desire. He was so beautiful, Romy wanted to cry.

She stroked his face, tracing a small scar on his cheek. "How did you get that?"

Blue smiled. "I wish I could tell you something cool, but I fell off my bike when I was a kid."

"That's not *un*cool."

"The bike still had training wheels. And I *still* fell off of it." Blue looked aggrieved as Romy started to laugh.

"Klutz. Sexy klutz, but still."

Blue shrugged, grinning. "I wasn't as suave as I am now."

Romy snorted. "Suave. You didn't realize at dinner two nights ago that you had marinara sauce all over your pretty face, Allende."

"I did. I was just hoping to entice you to lick it off."

"Ah," Romy nodded wisely. "You know me well, doctor."

"I know you well enough to know that food, any food, can charm you like a snake."

Romy kissed him as he looked smug. "Speaking of snake, put that incredible cock of yours back in me, boss."

Blue laughed. "Hmm, boss, I like that." He hitched her legs around his waist again, his cock already hard again. He slid into her and Romy sighed happily, winding her arms around his neck.

"You know, boss, if you like that … I'd be willing to be dominated … in bed. For you? God, yeah, that would be such a turn on."

He pinched her nipple hard and she yelped in surprise but it made her cunt flood with arousal. "Oh, you're wet, baby girl," Blue said, and slammed his cock deeper into her. They made love, clawing, biting, hungry for the other until they both came again, then, making sure their pagers were on, they wrapped their arms around one other and fell asleep.

Just after midnight, the door to the on-call room opened and Mac peered in, spotting them in the small puddle of light from the hallway. Romy heard the door open and she and Mac smiled at each other. Mac touched his hand over his heart and blew her a kiss, backing out of the room, and Romy felt safe and loved. *No one is going to take this away from me,* she thought, and closed her eyes, locked in the embrace of the man she loved.

DACRE HAD SEEN Romy go into the on-call room with Blue Allende and his gut had twisted with rage. He knew the police were looking for him but they had old photos of him, photos before he'd shaved his head and grown a thick beard, adding piercings, a neck tattoo, and thick spectacles. He'd bulked up too; it made the killings easier if they couldn't match his physical strength.

Gaius Eames had arranged the new identity so he could apply for the orderly job at Rainier Hope. Dacre still didn't trust the man; he wondered why he hated his half-brother so much when Gaius seemed to have unlimited resources. Maybe Gaius wanted Romy too, and if so, Dacre wouldn't stand for that. Romy was his. She hadn't even recognized him the time she'd asked him direct questions; she was friendly and polite, joking around with the patients and with him. He'd changed his voice too, whiskey and cigarettes lowering his register. No one, not even his damn parents, would recognize Dacre Mortimer, preppy Harvard grad, now.

Gaius Eames had asked of him one favor. "Don't kill your ex-wife yet," he'd said. "I want Blue to really fall for her so when she dies, he'll be destroyed."

Dacre gritted his teeth. "The thought of his hands on her ..."

Gaius had smiled. "Think of the ways you could punish her, Mortimer. Those girls you killed had it easy compared to what you're going to do to the lovely Romy."

Dacre had liked the sound of that, so he'd agreed. Working at the hospital was another one of Gaius's ideas as was the small studio apartment close to the hospital.

Now, as he heard the door of the on-call room click closed, he knew that Allende had his hands all over his Romy and it made him rage. Dacre checked his watch—his shift was over in five minutes. He paused, entertaining the fantasy of storming into the on-call room and butchering his ex-wife and her lover. Instead, he finished up his shift and left the hospital. His body tingled with rage and the need to kill. Gaius had told him his little game of killing women with Romy's initials had been found out—good, it meant she was scared.

Dacre went home, ate a sparse meal of microwave hot dogs, and sucked down a couple of beers. He watched TV mindlessly for a few hours, then, just after midnight, headed out into the city. He was careful always to wear black so that the blood of his victims would not show up on his clothes and when he returned home, he would seal those clothes into a sack and burn them in the furnace at work.

Tonight, he looked for anyone who resembled Romy. He found her working at a bar downtown, followed her when she closed up for the night, took her at the end of an alleyway, and dragged her into the darkness. She was beautiful, with long, dark, wavy hair, doe-eyed, petite. He overpowered her easily and as the knife sank deep into her flesh, Dacre felt the usual release. Staring at the girl unseeing, all he thought of was how it would feel to kill Romy like this, his blade slicing through her tender flesh, severing arteries, destroying her vital organs. This girl died too quickly, his knife cutting through her abdominal aorta clumsily, though he usually liked to draw it out.

He lowered her to the ground as she struggled for life, ripping her shirt open, and finishing her with a few brutal stabs. The girl, her eyes wide with terror and agony, made a gurgling sound as blood filled her throat, then went still. Dacre stood, breathing heavily, staring down at her, only seeing Romy's face on this girl's brutalized body.

Dacre sucked in lungfuls of air, smelling the rust-and-salt smell of his victim's blood, then, leaving her for others to find, walked slowly back home and feel into a deep, peaceful sleep.

CHAPTER 12

Stuart Eames looked up as his soon-to-be-ex-wife approached the table. He stood, dutifully kissing her on the cheek, and pulled out her chair for her. Hilary Eames smiled and sat down.

"Always the gentleman."

Stuart tried not to roll his eyes. Hilary was obviously in one of her seductive moods. "You look well, Hilary."

She smiled. "You too. Magda Sasse is obviously looking after you ... and I hear her daughter is looking after the Italian, too."

Stuart sighed. "His name is Blue as you well know, Hilary, and yes, he and Romy are seeing each other."

"Keeping it in the family."

He grimaced in disgust. "I didn't come here to talk about Blue's love life, Hilary. We agreed to meet to finalize the divorce, so shall we stick to that topic?"

Hilary smirked. Stuart studied her. Hilary had once been considered a beautiful woman, but now she was stick-thin, gaunt, brittle. Her dark hair, once her crowning glory, was now coiffed to hide the hairpieces she used to create the illusion of lustrousness, her blue eyes ringed with kohl, hard lines. Her full lips—enhanced by fillers—

made her look slightly ridiculous. Her cheekbones were jutting out and even the amount of make-up she wore couldn't conceal the greyness of her skin, the pinched look from denying herself food.

Being rich and thin was the overriding reason Hilary lived—that and to cause misery to those she felt envious of. Stuart wondered how he could ever have loved this woman; she was Magda's antithesis.

"So, you dropping your claim to the financial settlement has me wondering—what are you up to, Hilary?"

Hilary hid a smile behind her water glass. "I thought you'd be happy."

"Who is he? I know there must be a 'he' because otherwise there isn't a chance in hell you'd relinquish my money unless you had someone else lined up."

"You think so little of me?"

Stuart stayed silent rather than lie. Hilary shrugged. "Not that it's any of your business, Stuart, but Giles is ..."

"Giles?" Suddenly Stuart started to laugh. "You mean Giles St. Clement? *Lord* Giles St. Clement? Oh, Hilly, you really are so transparent."

Hilary's face contorted in anger. "If you must know, Giles and I are in love, and as soon as the divorce comes through, we are to be married."

"And you're moving to London? I can see it now. High tea with the prime minister as you peddle your faux-manitarian causes. Blow jobs abound and suddenly, Lady St. Clement, you're receiving titles of your own. Honorary damehoods, perhaps?"

Stuart hadn't meant to be so cutting—it wasn't his style, and this meeting was, after all, to make sure Hilary did sign the divorce papers —and now he realized he had gone too far. Hilary's eyes glittered with spite.

"What's it to you who I marry, or who I 'blow,' as you so crudely put it? This is what I want, Stuart, just like your pathetic little hippie is who you want. Aren't you glad I'll be out of your life for good?"

Stuart shrugged. "Sure ... I just hope Giles knows what he's let himself in for."

"Fuck you, Stuart. I never loved you; I was stupid to think I did."

Stuart's smile faded. "You think I don't know that? And you made Bianca's life a misery too."

"She spawned your precious lovechild, the saint-like Blue. If you only knew, Stuart, about your bastard son."

"What the hell is that supposed to mean?" Stuart was irked now but Hilary just smiled.

"You have two sons, Stuart. Isn't it about time you concentrated on your firstborn? Gaius tells me he feels shut out of your new family."

"That's not even close to true, Hilary. Gaius just tells you what you want to hear, because it suits him to feel like the redheaded stepchild. Magda has made great efforts to include him. Far more efforts than you made with Blue."

"You're just surrounded by saint-like people, aren't you?"

Stuart gritted his teeth. This was more like the Hilary he knew—spiteful, resentful, vindictive. "I really think we should stick to signing these papers. Do you want lunch, Hilary?"

She shook her head, dismissive. "I don't have time." She took the papers from him and scrawled her signature where he indicated. Stuart put the signed papers back in his jacket pocket.

"Thank you. I wish you well, Hilary."

Hilary smiled at him and for a brief second, Stuart could see the beautiful woman she had once been. Then the malice crept back in her face. "Tell your girlfriend's daughter to watch out for Blue ... he isn't what he says he is."

Hilary's last words were still bugging Stuart as he drove back to Magda's home. They had decided that he would move in with her after the wedding, selling his massive condo. "I don't need it," he'd told her, "this is home to me now."

Magda saw the preoccupation on his face and Stuart told her

what Hilary had said. Magda shrugged it off. "She's just trying to upset you. Blue is a good man; we all know that."

Stuart sighed. "I know. I just don't trust Hilary not to go screw things up for him. She loathed Bianca, and barely even spoke to Blue —until, get this, until he was a young teenager and started to blossom into his looks. Then she would show him off like a trophy. Blue isn't like Gaius. He hated being paraded around like a prize. As soon as he was eighteen, he left home, just to get away from her. I confess, I helped him move out." He sat and rubbed his face, but then smiled at Magda. "But all that aside, she signed the papers."

Magda grinned and sat down on his knees. "You're a free man?"

"I'm a free man ... so, officially, Magdalena Helen Sasse ... would you do me the great honor of marrying me?"

Magda laughed, and nodded. "I will, Stuart Gregory Eames. I really will ... and if you'll have me, on Christmas Day."

Stuart grinned, knowing the arrangements were almost in place for their wedding. He kissed her tenderly, gazing up into her navy-blue eyes. "I can't wait, my darling. I can't wait."

Romy was concentrating so hard on the practice dummy she was performing a surgery on that she didn't see Mac sidle into the room until he poked her side and made her jump. "Dude! You just killed my patient."

Mac laughed. "Nah, she was a goner anyway. So ..."

Romy hid a grin. "Yes?"

"You and Doc Allende?"

Romy flushed, but smiled. "Pretty much."

"How long?"

"A couple of months."

"Rom?" She looked up to see his smile. "Is it love?"

She nodded, flushing again. "It is. I'm crazy about him."

"Good. You get your man, girl. It's not like it's a huge surprise to anyone."

Romy looked at him sharply. "What?"

Mac held his hands up. "Slow your roll. I didn't tell anyone. But the chemistry between the two of you speaks for itself."

He watched her for a few minutes as she worked. "Rom? Did you hear? More murders."

Romy's hand slipped and she cussed, ripping off her gloves to see the small gash in the top of her finger. Mac helped her to clean it up. "Girl, why were you wearing gloves to operate on a dummy?"

"Habit," she said, "ouch."

"Sorry. Look, it just needs cleaning and a stitch is all. No biggie. Want me to do it?"

"Please."

Mac studied her face as he helped her. "I know you think these killings are your fault. They're not, babe. They are the work of a very sick, very bad man. Do you know how many times I thank God that he didn't kill you that day? And I didn't even know you back then. You're a survivor, Romy."

"But what does that mean when innocent women are being killed because of me?"

"It's not because of you!" Mac said angrily. "God, I could kill Dacre Mortimer with my bare hands. Have the police told you anything about their search?"

Romy shook her head. "He could be anywhere, Mac."

"Except here. We have his picture up at every entrance, all the security team has been advised to look out, all the reception staff."

"I know, and I'm grateful. Thanks, Mac."

He finished treating her finger. "You deserve happy, Romy. We can all see that you and Blue make each other happy. Live that, not the past."

Romy hugged her friend. "Thanks, Mac."

ROMY WENT to find Blue afterward, eager to see him and kiss him but as she approached his office door, she could hear him arguing. "No ... no way. I do not want to see you or talk to you. Why can't you get that into your head?"

Romy stopped, listening but she couldn't hear anyone replying. It must be a phone call. Feeling guilty, she hovered just outside the door. She heard him sigh. "Look, I don't know why you're bringing this up now. Perhaps you heard I'm in love with someone else? I thought so. Keep your less-than-subtle threats and go fuck yourself." She heard him slam the phone down and mutter to himself. Romy waited a beat then knocked at his door.

Blue looked up and for a second, his face was stormy, dark, beautiful—and terrifying. When he realized who it was, the storm cleared and he grinned at her. "Why are you knocking, baby? Come here."

Romy went into his arms and he kissed her tenderly, his eyes never leaving hers. "God, I love you, woman."

Romy chuckled. "Right back at you. I just came to see the schedule of surgeries—and to kiss your face off, of course.

"Of course." He pulled her onto his lap and reached for the schedule. "Light, today, unless we get any emergencies." He stroked her hair back from her face. "After the lap, you could duck out and go Christmas shopping if you want. I'll cover."

"Nah. That's what Amazon.com is for." Romy leaned her cheek against his and closed her eyes. She was so curious as to who he had been talking to, but couldn't bring herself to ask. "I did some serious shopping at lunch. Speaking of which ... I have no idea what to get you."

"All I need is you, baby." Blue kissed her. "If I have you, I have everything."

Romy grinned. "Mushy. Okay, so I'll ask your dad."

"Like he'll know. Honestly, Romy, I don't need anything." He twirled a lock of her hair around his finger. "How about this? Instead of exchanging gifts, we go away together after Christmas."

Romy smiled. "Is this you trying to get me out of Seattle again?"

"A little," Blue admitted with a wry smile. "But also, I keep dreaming of us in a rustic Italian villa, making love in the olive groves. My fantasy is you in a summer dress, no underwear, and me fucking you against a cypress tree, my cock buried deep in your silky cunt, my fingers stroking your clit, my tongue in your mouth ..."

Romy, turned on, groaned. "God, Blue ..."

Grinning wickedly, he snaked his hand into her top, pulling it down over one breast, sliding the lacy cup of her bra down and taking her nipple into his mouth. His other hand slid slowly up her thigh, under her skirt, caressing her through her increasingly damp panties, then slipping underneath to stroke her clit. "I'll fuck you so hard that the whole of Tuscany will hear you come, beautiful girl."

Romy buried her head in his neck. "Blue ... God, I'm so wet for you."

In a flash he had swept her onto the couch, locked the door, and flicked the light off. The whole back wall of his office was glass and Romy glanced quickly to see if anyone could see in. Blue grinned down at her as he unzipped his pants and tugged her underwear off. "Maybe we'll get caught, baby."

His smile, his words, sent a thrill through her and he plunged his ramrod-hard cock into her and they fucked deliriously, not caring if they were caught. Romy sighed as she came, feeling him pumping his seed deep inside her. "God, we're such a pair of sex fiends."

Blue chuckled. "Yes, we are."

Laughing and talking, they tidied themselves up and went back to work. The routine laparotomy went easily and afterwards, Blue took Romy out to dinner.

ROMY DIDN'T KNOW when she started to feel uneasy, but in the car on the way home, she kept looking behind them, as if she had seen something. Blue frowned at her. "You okay, baby?"

Romy nodded, but her chest was tight. "I don't know why but I feel like ... someone was watching us."

"In my office?"

She shook her head. "No, at the restaurant. I went to the bathroom, and I could have sworn ... no, never mind. I'm just being paranoid." She glanced behind them again.

Blue looked in the rearview mirror. "Sweetheart, if your instincts are telling you something, we should listen to them. Do you think we're being followed?"

Romy didn't want to sound insane but Blue's expression was serious. "It's crazy, but yes. There's a dark sedan that's been following us all the way from the restaurant."

"Gotcha." With deftness and skill, Blue pulled the car off the freeway and onto a side street. He made a circuit of the almost deserted business district, and then circled back towards his apartment. "How about now?"

Romy was watching carefully. "I can't see it anymore. I'm sorry, honey, maybe I was imagining it."

"Better safe than not."

She smiled gratefully at him. "I promise I'm not a hysterical female."

Blue laughed. "Would never have crossed my mind that you were."

As they parked the car in the garage beneath his building, Romy couldn't resist checking out the other cars there. Blue grinned at her. "Still being super spy?"

"You got me."

He took her hand. "Come on, Black Widow, let's go home and cuddle some."

In the elevator, alone, he kissed her tenderly. "You know, if you want, we could look for somewhere together. We don't have to stay here."

"I love your apartment," she said, leaning into him, feeling his arms tightening around her. She reached down and squeeze his cock through his jeans and he grinned.

"Insatiable."

"You know it."

He was still laughing when he unlocked the door to his apartment and held it for her. "After you, ma'am."

Romy's laughter echoed through the hallway but when she got into the living room, her smile faded. She heard Blue cuss behind her.

"What the fuck?"

The naked dark-haired woman slowly spread her legs with a wide smile on her face. "Hello, darling Blue. Is this your new toy? Would she like to play with us?"

Romy's whole body was icy cold. She slowly turned to Blue. "I take it back. I hate your apartment."

She pushed past him, wrenching her arm free when he grabbed it. "No, baby, wait, this isn't what it—"

But Romy ran, slamming the door behind her, her sobs wracking and desiccating.

HILARY EAMES STOOD up and sashayed over to her stepson. "Flighty, isn't she?"

Blue, his anger threatening to overwhelm him, glowered at her. "What the fuck do you think you're doing, Hilary?"

She touched his cheek and he flinched away. She smiled. "Just reclaiming what is mine, Blue."

"Get *out.*" Blue clenched his fists to stop himself from physically hauling her out of his apartment. "Now, Hilary, and don't ever come back."

Hilary pretended to pout. "Come on. Don't you remember the fun we used to have? God, you were like a Roman god back then." She studied him. "Now ... you look tired, Blue. She's exhausting you, making you pretend that you're good enough for her when you and I know differently, don't we?"

"Get out now, Hilary, or I won't be responsible for what I'll do."

Hilary smirked. "Fine. I'll go. You know where to call me."

"Don't hold your breath. You know what you did to me. Don't pretend it was anything more than ..." Blue squeezed his eyes shut, trying to erase the memories, the feelings from back when he was just a kid.

"Call it what you will, Blue." Hilary reached down and squeezed his groin. "You may tell one story, but your magnificent cock told another."

Blue did lose his temper then, and taking her by the upper arm, hauled Hilary to the door and threw her out. A bright flash blinded him, and he realized that a paparazzo had been waiting outside his door to take a photo of him throwing a naked and grinning Hilary from his home.

But Romy was all he could think about, out there, unprotected. Blue called the security firm. "Find her. Protect her. She won't want to see me at the moment and that's fine. But, please, keep her safe."

"Will do, boss."

CHAPTER 13

Running out into the midnight streets, Romy kept going until she could not breathe any longer. Stopping, dragging much needed oxygen into her lungs, she allowed herself to feel the pain of what had just happened in and it bent her double. "God ... *God.*"

Slowly, as her breathing returned to normal, she began to walk, dazed. She knew it wasn't safe to do this but at this moment, the pain of Blue's betrayal seemed to overwhelm any fear that Dacre might catch up with her.

Come for me now, Dacre, and end this pain for me. I don't care anymore.

She sat down on a low wall and put her head in her hands, willing the tears to stop.

God, how stupid was I? To think a man like Blue wouldn't have a fleet of women in his past. How long ago had he slept with this one? Who the fuck was she? She was beautiful, if skinny as hell, but way too old for him. Jesus, that's what you're focusing on, Sasse?

Fuck. Romy wiped her eyes. She'd call a cab and get them to pick her up at the end of the street. She was dialing when a silver Audi pulled up beside her. She began to walk quicker, nervous now.

"Romy?"

She stopped, turning towards the speaker. Gaius smiled at her. "What on earth are you doing out here so late?"

"I ..." Romy didn't know what to say. "Blue was called in for an emergency and I decided to try and find a cab." Lame as hell.

"Girl, get in. With your rabid ex on the loose, you really do not need to be out on the streets alone."

"I'm fine." Her voice shook, betraying her. Gaius got out and came to her.

"Come on, sweetheart. I'll take you home."

Romy let him put her in his passenger seat and drive away from Blue's neighborhood. Gaius looked over at her, concerned.

"Are you okay?"

Romy nodded. "Would you mind taking me to my sister's place? To Artemis's place?" She gave him the address and then smiled tentatively at him. "Thanks, Gaius."

"It's no problem ... but are you sure you're okay? You look upset."

"I'm fine."

"You said that already."

Romy gave a half-hearted laugh. "Just tired."

She stared out of the car window. The shock was dissipating now, and Romy was beginning to regret running away. She should have stood her ground and gone toe to toe with the whore in Blue's flat. Romy gritted her teeth. Then again, why the hell hadn't Blue come after her?

Was it the guilt of being caught? God. Romy closed her eyes. The pain in her chest was killing her. Had she gotten him so wrong?

No. She was sure of Blue's love for her, utterly sure. There had to be some kind of rational explanation for it.

Gaius left her alone on the journey, only turning to her as they turned into Artemis's street. "Are you sure I can't do anything else for you, Romy?"

"No, thank you again, Gaius." A thought occurred to her. "What were you doing in Blue's neighborhood tonight?"

"Just hoping to see my brother for a few minutes. Nothing

important."

That didn't ring true, but Romy didn't have the energy to press the point. She got out, then bent down to thank him again.

Gaius smiled at her. "It's no problem. If you need anything, I'm always here for you, Romy. Always."

She watched him drive away, then dug in her purse for the key. All of the sisters had keys to each other's houses and Romy was glad she wouldn't have to wake Arti up. She snuck into the house, but halfway up the stairs her phone beeped. She knew it had to be Blue.

Baby, where are you? I swear it wasn't how it looked—but of course I would say that. Please believe me, her being here was nothing to do with us. Please just let me know you're safe. I love you.

Romy sighed, all her anger dissipated.

We'll talk tomorrow, Blue. That's all I can promise right now. I'm at Arti's for the night. I'm safe.

Of course. Just know I love you.

I love you too. Tomorrow.

Tomorrow.

Romy climbed up the stairs wearily, and slipped into Arti's guest bedroom. She stripped down to her underwear and into bed—only to encounter bare flesh. She shrieked, as did the other person in the bed, and Romy skittered across the room to switch the light on.

A young woman with dark hair and huge brown eyes was staring at her, her hand clamped over her mouth.

"Who are you?" Romy asked, breathless, but the girl didn't have time to answer before Artemis burst into the room, followed by a giant of a man who looked familiar. Romy gaped at him. "Dan? Dan Helmond?"

The man grinned widely, a strange counterpoint to the three women all in shock. "Romy Sasse, as I live and breathe. I take it you've met my daughter and your mini-me, Octavia. Tavia, meet Romy Sasse, Artemis's sister."

Romy and her younger double stared at each other for a long moment before Romy, not knowing what else to do, burst out laughing.

CHAPTER 14

Romy shrugged, recounting the story to her sister. "So I just walked out. Wouldn't you?"

Artemis, sitting opposite her sister at the breakfast bar, chewed on her toast thoughtfully. "Maybe. No, probably not. You know me, I would have demanded a full and detailed explanation."

"With color-coding."

Artemis grinned as Dan and Octavia laughed. "And, you, sis, are the firebrand, so I guess I can't blame you for walking away."

Romy sighed. "I told Blue I'd meet him this morning in the city. Don't suppose you could give me a ride?"

"I can." Octavia said, spooning the last of her cereal into her mouth, "I have to go to the library, it's no problem."

Romy grinned at her. "Thanks, dude. I still can't get over how alike we look. Daniel, are you sure you didn't fool around with my mom when we were back in high school?"

The women laughed as Dan held up his hands. "All I'm saying is Magda is a beautiful woman."

"Dad! God, you're so embarrassing." Octavia hid her face in her hands as her father smirked.

Romy snorted with laughter and poked Octavia. "Come on then, twinsie, let's get going."

ON THE DRIVE into the city, Romy and Octavia chatted easily, then Octavia smiled at her.

"Artemis told me you are actually a twin. I'm sorry about your brother."

Romy felt a lump in her throat. "Thanks ... I miss him still, even though it's been over twenty years."

"What happened? If you don't mind telling me."

Romy cleared her throat. "Not at all." Her voice quivered a little but she ignored it. "It was so quick, such a normal moment in a normal day. He fell over in the school yard. He was playing with some friends and tripped and hit his head. For a few hours he was okay, and then the next morning, Mom found him dead in bed from a hemorrhage."

Even now, Romy remembered the agony of seeing her twin, the person closest to her, blue- lipped and lifeless.

Octavia had tears in her eyes. "I'm so sorry, Romy."

"You know what it's like to lose someone, Tavia. It never gets easier; you just get used to the pain."

Octavia nodded. "I know. Mom fought cancer twice, once before she had me. That time she won, and was determined that it wouldn't stop her and Dad from having kids. They went through seven rounds of IVF before one took. Sometimes I wonder if having me, putting her body through all of that, made her weaker and allowed the cancer back in."

Romy squeezed her hand. "No, honey, it doesn't work like that. And, believe me, she would have taken the cancer over and over again if it meant having you in her life."

Octavia looked tearful. "Thank you, Romy." She laughed a little through her tears. "I wish you *were* my sister."

"How about we pretend we are? After all, it looks like Arti and your dad are pretty much solid—so that makes you family. Of course,

I would technically be your step-aunt—but sister sounds better, right?"

Octavia grinned at Romy. "Deal."

OCTAVIA DROPPED Romy off at the breakfast place and waved goodbye. Romy drew in a deep lungful of oxygen and went inside, seeing Blue was already waiting for her. His green eyes were troubled, wary, but Romy allowed him to pull her into a hug. "Thank you for coming, baby."

Romy leaned into him, breathing in his woodsy, clean scent. "Let's talk."

They ordered eggs and toast with strong black coffee and Romy waited. Blue looked at her. "I have no idea how she got into my apartment, but I swear to you, Romy, I'm not sleeping with her."

"Who is she?"

Blue hesitated. "An ex-patient who got a little too close."

"Did you sleep with her before you knew me?" Romy was watching his expression carefully. *Don't lie, please don't lie.*

Again, Blue paused. "It's more complicated than that."

His answer irked Romy. "Either you had sex with her or not, Blue."

His expression was unreadable then in a low voice. "Technically, I did have intercourse with her."

"What does that mean?"

"Romy ... I have a past, and some things are too painful, too scarring to discuss. You should know that."

Ouch. "Don't try and weasel out of this by bringing up Dacre, Blue."

"I'm not trying to weasel out of anything. It is what it is."

Romy sighed. She wanted to believe Blue, but there was something in her gut instinct making it difficult. "But you're no longer involved with her?"

"No, nor any other woman. Believe me, Romy, you are my love, my life." He leaned forward and brushed her lips with his. She didn't pull away. "Nothing will ever change that. As far as I'm concerned, you and me? We're endgame."

Romy felt a rush of warmth inside her at his words. "We are?"

"*Yes.*" This time his words were defiant, determined. Blue held her gaze steadily. "I love you."

Romy half smiled. "I love you too, Doc."

"Can we move past this?"

She considered for a long moment then nodded. "I guess we can. But no more beautiful naked women in the apartment."

Blue grinned. "Unless it's you."

Romy laughed then, her tension falling away. "Unless it's me. And get your locks changed, would you? If she could get in that easily, anyone could."

"Already done," he said grimly, "And the building's security team got a tongue-lashing as well."

"Maybe we should look for somewhere together."

Blue nodded. "I'd like that. I want to be somewhere of both our choosing."

Romy was dreaming now. "Maybe out on one of the islands? I ..." Her attention was suddenly caught by the flat screen TV in the corner of the diner. Blue's face flashed up, followed by a photograph of the naked woman being thrown out of his apartment, and Blue's shocked, angry face behind her. With a sledgehammer-like shock to her heart, Romy read the headline.

PROMINENT SEATTLE SURGEON *in late-night tryst with naked stepmother, socialite Hilary Eames. Photographer captures moment lover's tiff escalates into public humiliation.*

ROMY FELT her throat fill with vomit. "Oh my God ..." She breathed and turned on a shocked Blue. "An ex-patient, huh? You sick, perverted *fuck ... Jesus*, Blue, your own stepmother?"

"It wasn't like that, I swear." Blue's voice was gravelly, broken, his shoulders slumped, but Romy had no sympathy.

"How could you?" She didn't wait for an answer but darted to the bathrooms and threw up and up until she was sobbing and dry-heaving. She sat on the bathroom floor and cried, her heart shattering. *What the fuck is wrong with the world?*

A young waitress came to find her. "Are you okay?"

Romy shook her head. "No."

"Your friend asked me to come see if you were okay." The waitress crouched down beside her, her kind face concerned. Romy tried to smile.

"He's no friend of mind." She wiped her face. "Is there a back way out of this place?"

The waitress led Romy through the kitchens and Romy thanked her, pressing a large tip into her hands. "Give me a few moments before you tell him I'm gone, would you?"

"Of course. I hope you're okay."

"Thanks, honey."

ROMY WENT OUT into the cold December streets and walked to work. How the hell were they going to resolve this? Everything was so fucked up. *You should never have slept with him to begin with.* Would she have to transfer to a different hospital? *God.*

She was in the locker room when Mac came and hugged her. "You okay? I saw the crap on the news."

"No, I'm not okay, but I have to work, so ... here I am." She lowered her voice. "Is he here? Have you seen him?"

Mac nodded, glancing around at the other residents. "He looks broken, Romy. Utterly devastated. I saw him talking to Quinto."

"You defending him?"

"No way. Team Romy all the way. I'm just saying, he's not out there preening."

Romy felt a little better and a little worse at that. She almost wanted Blue to be unrepentant so she could keep being mad at him.

He was sleeping with his stepmother, she told herself, you *have plenty to be mad about*. A few minutes later, just as they were leaving for rounds, the Chief of Surgery, Beau Quinto, came to find them.

"Okay, people, so a bit of news. Doctor Allende has requested and been granted some personal time. Therefore, I'll be your lead for the time being. Sasse and Jones, if you could still keep to the general surgical schedule you had planned, I'll be stepping in to replace Doctor Allende."

Quinto's eyes flicked to Romy's face briefly and she couldn't read the expression. Was he mad at her? She bristled then told herself to calm down. The man was a professional—and she hadn't done anything wrong.

Quinto gave out his orders to the rest of the residents and they all scattered throughout the hospital. Romy was relieved that she had some breathing space. Mac nudged her as they walked down the OR's. "Wonder how long Allende will be away."

She shrugged. "Until he gets his life sorted out."

"Does that include you?"

Romy didn't know how to answer him.

CHAPTER 15

Christmas Eve, and Romy finished late in the evening, wanting to catch up with her files before she took some time away for her mother's wedding. If she was honest, she was delaying going home. Going home meant facing Blue for the first time since the Hilary incident, but there was no way out of it. In the morning, her mother would marry Stuart, and there was no way either she or Blue would let their parents down.

Maybe we should just shake hands and live as step-siblings, she thought now. The thought depressed her, though, and she suddenly felt tearful. *Distraction is what I need.*

She walked through the floor, checking on all her post-surgical patients, chatting to the few who were still awake, wishing them a Merry Christmas even if it was spent away from their families. The hospital always made sure that, if at all possible, they could have an enjoyable time. There was one patient who wouldn't even know it was Christmas. Kelly Yang, a young woman who had been in a car accident a few weeks previously, lay in a coma. No family, no visitors, and so Romy had taken to sitting with her, holding her hand, and talking to her, trying to reach into the young woman's locked-in mind.

"Hey, Kels," Romy said now, pulling a chair up to the side of her bed. "How you doing, kiddo?" She checked Kelly's vital signs, flicked her light in the girl's eyes, then sat down. "Merry Christmas, sweetheart. Wish you were awake to share it, but I promise, when you do wake up, I'll make sure you have your Christmas."

She sat with Kelly nearly an hour, almost falling asleep, when she heard someone at the doorway. "How is she?"

Romy turned to see one of the orderlies, a huge, hulking man, nodding at Kelly. He was bald-headed with a thick dark beard, multiple piercings and thick spectacles, but his smile was friendly. Romy wracked her brain for his name. Wally? Warren?

"The same," she replied, looking back at Kelly, "although I live in hope she'll wake up."

"Fingers crossed. Sorry to bother you, doc, but we just needed to check in, see if you needed us anymore tonight."

Romy smiled at him. "No, thanks ... Warren. Have a good Christmas."

"You too, Doc. Thanks."

Left alone again, Romy squeezed Kelly's hand. "Do me a favor, kiddo. Give me the best Christmas gift by waking up, huh? Sweet dreams, sweetheart."

THE HOSPITAL WAS SO QUIET, so still, that as Romy walked through the reception area out to the parking lot, her heels echoed on the polished floor. Outside, the temperature was dropping fast and thick, fluffy snow falling from the sky. *A picture-perfect Christmas for us,* Romy thought, pulling out of the lot and turning the car towards her mother's house. The roads were almost empty as the snow began to thicken, and Romy drove with extra care, her heart thumping painfully all the way home.

When she got home, she only saw one light on—Artemis' old room. Breathing a sigh of relief that everyone else seemed to be in bed, she snuck through the house to her old room. Juno, back from New Orleans, was curled up in one side of the bed, fast asleep.

Romy pulled her wet boots and jeans off, changing into her fluffy brushed cotton jammies and pulling her robe around her. Despite the time, she wasn't tired, and so, instead of waking Juno up with her restlessness, Romy tugged a comforter from the closet and went back downstairs. The living room had been transformed into a winter wonderland by her mother, thousands of tiny white lights, white ribbons, and tasteful Christmas decorations everywhere.

It really is going to be a fairytale wedding, Romy thought, with a pang of both sadness and joy. Her mother deserved every happiness and now Romy nodded to herself. She would not let this thing with Blue ruin her mom's day. She would tell him they could talk—after the wedding. In the meantime, they would plaster smiles on their faces and be a family.

She felt, rather than heard, the person behind her. Romy turned to see Blue, shirtless, barefoot, and in jeans, staring at her. In the blue light of the early hours, he looked like an apparition. His eyes were wide and sad. Romy gazed back at him for a long moment, then slowly pulled her top over her head, releasing the drawstring on her pants and stepping out of them.

Wordlessly, he came to her, hesitant at first, then as his cold hands touched her skin, she shivered with desire and he crushed his lips against hers. Romy could not help but sink into the embrace, her longing for him almost debilitating. Her hands went to the fly of his jeans and soon he too was naked, his cock standing proud against his belly, quivering as she stroked it. There was a question in Blue's eyes and Romy answered it with just a nod. She lay down on the couch and opened her arms to him.

Blue went into them, hitching her legs around his waist and thrusting into her in one long, quick movement. Romy gasped as he filled her, her cunt contracting around his cock, moving with him as they made love. Romy did not think of anything else at that moment but of her own needs, her desire for the man in her arms.

Blue held her gaze as he braced himself and moved quicker, harder, deeper, Romy tilting her hips up to take him in as deep as she could. Blue's thrusts were almost violent now, making Romy's hips burn as he slammed his cock into her. He was angry, Romy could tell, but right now, she wanted that anger, needed it to fuel her own. Blue came inside her, burying his face in her neck as he groaned, his cum pumping out of him, filling her belly. Romy dug her fingernails into his buttocks as she too reached her climax, gasping and moaning softly.

Afterward they gazed at each other. "I hate how much I love you," she said, and he nodded.

"I promise, Romy, I will make this right between us. We need to talk."

"I know," Romy closed her eyes as he kissed her throat. "But after the wedding."

"Agreed. I love you, Romy," he said, his voice trembling with emotion. "I've never loved anyone or anything as much as I love you, beautiful girl. Please don't ever leave me."

Romy was moved beyond words and hot tears dripped from her eyes, splashing on her naked body. Blue stroked her face, wiped away her tears. "I promise, I'll tell you everything. *Everything.* There will be no more secrets between us."

Blue lifted her into his arms and carried her upstairs to the guestroom. They entangled their limbs, in a bid to get as close as possible, lips on lips, belly to belly, her soft breasts pressed up against his hard chest, and fell asleep together.

Romy's last thought before she gave into sleep was that maybe, just maybe, everything would be all right.

GAIUS HAD WATCHED his step-brother and Romy make love, his hand down his own shorts, jerking off, as he gazed at Romy's spectacular naked body. She was so beautiful that Gaius thought it would almost be a shame when Dacre Mortimer killed her. What a waste ... then again, the thought of seeing her confused and in agony as Mortimer murdered her was also a turn-on. If Dacre could see them now, Gaius thought with a smile. Romy riding Blue, her large, pillowy breasts moving in rhythm, her flat belly soft and sensual. Gaius imagined putting a bullet into it as she rode Blue, watching the horror in his hated stepbrother's face as she bled out on top of him.

He muffled his grunt of release, wiping his hand on a bunch of tissues. *God* ... he would love to fuck Romy before she died, but what would the insanely jealous Mortimer do if he did? End him? Probably. No, he would have to settle for voyeurism when it came to the middle Sasse sister. The more important thing was that Blue was destroyed ... Gaius gritted is teeth. When he had seen that photograph of Blue throwing Gaius' naked mother out of his apartment, the rage had been like nothing he'd ever known.

Gaius had been so mad that he had ignored his mother's phone calls, staying silent as she'd begged outside his door.

How could you, Mom? With the man I have hated all my life ... fucking whore.

Gaius watched now as Blue swept Romy into his arms and gritted his teeth. *You took the woman I loved, brother, and now I'm going to do the same to you. Romy is a dead woman, Blue, and you know what?*

It's entirely your fault.

CHAPTER 16

Romy woke feeling more at peace that she'd expected to. Blue's arms were around her and she stayed locked in them as she gazed up at him. Yes, she loved this man. Whatever he had done in the past was the past. He'd said he would tell her everything, and she believed him.

Romy was amazed at herself. After Dacre, she had struggled with trust, and yet here she was risking her heart once again for this man.

As they dressed for the wedding later, Romy smiled at him. "Damn, man, you wear a suit well."

He was wearing a dark gray, exquisitely tailored suit which brought out the green of his eyes. He was grinning at her. "Woman, you should see what I'm seeing."

The dark gold shift dress clung to her curves, simple in its design but perfectly matched to her olive skin tone. The lightest makeup and her dark hair falling in waves down her back completed her bridesmaid look. Blue couldn't keep his hands off of her, kissing her tenderly.

She stroked his face. "Blue, today is all about Mom and Stuart. That's all I care about today, so let's put everything else aside for after they've left for their honeymoon."

"I agree ... but can I just say one thing?"

"Go for it."

"I love you, Romy Sasse, and there are things in my past I'm ashamed of, but nothing, nothing means more to me than earning and deserving your love and your trust."

DOWNSTAIRS, Artemis was arranging everything and everyone and Romy saw that some of the guests had started to arrive. She welcomed them in and made sure they had drinks before heading up to see how Magda was doing.

Her mother was uncharacteristically calm. "Hello, darling. Could you help me with this hair comb?"

Magda was dressed in a simple pale cream dress too, with only some ornate beading around the neck and sleeves. The hair comb was encrusted with rubies—a present from Romy's grandmother when Magda had graduated from college.

"You look breathtaking, Mom." Romy hugged her gingerly and Magda beamed. She studied her daughter.

"You look happier, darling. Did you and Blue talk?"

Romy half-smiled. "A little. But today isn't about us, it's about you and Stuart. As the reckless middle daughter, I think it's probably up to me to ask the awkward question. Are you sure, Mom?"

Her mother met her gaze steadily. "I am, Romy. I truly am."

Romy smiled. "Then I wish you nothing but utter happiness and joy forever. I love Stuart; he really is a good man. Oh, here. Dad sent a message too."

"He did?" Magda read the card James Sasse had sent. "That's sweet. Your daddy is a good man, Romy. In spite of everything"

"I know, Mom. And now I have a stepdad too."

Magda laughed. "Not quite yet." She glanced at her clock. "Wow, that came around quickly. Forty-five minutes and then the nerve-wracking stuff will be over with and we can party."

. . .

A HALF-HOUR LATER, Romy walked her mother down the wooden staircase and to the front of the aisle, Artemis serving as matron of honor, and a grinning Juno, resplendent in a man's tuxedo, welcoming the guests to the wedding.

Blue and Gaius stood at Stuart's side as he married Magda, Blue's eyes twinkling with happiness as he winked at Romy.

God, I love you, she thought as she smiled back, and felt the weight of the last few weeks fall away from her. This was all that mattered, love, family, celebration. As Magda and Stuart said their vows, she wondered idly if she and Blue would ever get here. She didn't even know if he regarded marriage as a goal. Romy never had—until she'd met Blue.

Her mother looked so overwhelmingly happy that as Juno declared them husband and wife, Romy burst into tears, making everyone laugh.

THE RECEPTION WAS a laidback affair of chatting, casual speeches which made everyone laugh, soft music, and a buffet of such delicious food that it was soon gone and the caterers were thanked and sent on their way.

Blue sat with Romy on his lap in one of the armchairs. Juno sprawled on the sofa, one of their guests' toddler asleep in her arms. Artemis, Dan, and Octavia sat on the carpet, teasing each other.

Romy watched her mother circulate the room, taking time to chat with every guest, introducing them to her new husband. Blue grinned at Romy. "Some of Dad's friends are maybe a little too ..."

"Snooty?"

Blue laughed. "I was going to say reserved, but snooty works. They can't figure out what they're supposed to do in such a relaxed gathering."

Romy shrugged and snuggled into his arms. Blue pressed his lips to her forehead. "Romy?"

"Yes, baby?"

"Will you come to Italy with me for New Year's?"

Romy looked up at him. "Blue, we need to resolve things between us first."

"I know, I'm just saying ... we'll talk today, tomorrow, maybe the next day. It's going to be hard for me to talk about some of this stuff. So, I just thought, if, and I mean, if, no pressure, if we can reach a resolution—let's have a few days of us, away from all of this."

Romy kissed his neck. "How soon do I have to confirm?"

"A couple of days."

She nodded. "Then, once Stuart and Mom leave for honeymoon, let's go back to your apartment and lock ourselves in and get through this. I want to go with you, baby, I really do, but not until everything is out in the open."

"That's fair." He pressed his lips to hers. "I love you."

MAGDA HUGGED HER DAUGHTERS, tears flooding down her face. "I love you, Arti, Romulus, and JunoBoo. So much. Thank you for making my day so perfect, so beautiful."

Stuart, himself moved deeply, also embraced them. "I will never replace your dad but just know—to me, you are already my daughters, and I think myself the luckiest man on Earth."

Even the stoic Artemis was crying as they waved them off.

"God, Barbados for a month ..." groaned a jealous Juno. Octavia giggled with her; the two of them already fast friends. "Come on, people, let's ignore the tidying up and go drink the contents of Mom's liquor cabinet."

ROMY AND BLUE excused themselves and drove through the cold night back to the city, making it to Blue's apartment just after midnight. Blue opened the door for her, and Romy couldn't help but brace herself for another unwanted intrusion. This time though, they were totally alone.

They sat down at his kitchen table, Blue finding a bottle of scotch and some glasses and pouring a finger of the dark tan liquid into each.

"So," he began and Romy took his hand.

"So."

Blue breathed in a deep lungful of oxygen. "Hilary Eames. Hilary Eames is a vindictive, manipulative piece of human excrement. We all know that. That's not all she is. She ..." His voice broke and he looked away from Romy's gaze. "She likes young men, Romy. *Very* young men."

It took Romy a second to catch on, and her heart sank. "Oh, God."

"Yep. After Mom died, after I came to live with Stuart, at first, she wouldn't even look at me. Then, one night, when I was fifteen, she came to my room late at night, just in her robe."

Romy didn't say anything, swallowing over the lump in her throat. Blue gave her a humorless smile. "That night, she didn't do anything but stroke my face, tell me what a handsome boy I was. How I looked like a carved statue in one of Italy's great palaces. The next day, she went back to ignoring me. Then a couple of weeks later, she came to my room when I was asleep and got in beside me. I woke to find her ... sucking my penis. I was fifteen."

"Oh, no ..." Romy was horrified.

Blue looked desolate. "Of course, she told me if I told anyone, she would deny it and I would be cast out with nothing and nobody. The next night, she put my hand on her genitals and told me to stroke her. I did, because I was so terrified of her."

Romy's tears were flooding down her face. "Oh my God, Blue, I'm so sorry ..."

"She raped me for the first time three weeks shy of my sixteenth birthday. By then, she had threatened me so many times that I was a shadow of my former self. I was completely under her control. I still can't smell her perfume without being taken back there. The last time was when I was eighteen, just before I went to Harvard. She knew she was losing control over me, and so was even more threatening. She would have me killed if I told anybody. I didn't doubt she had both the means and the viciousness to do so."

He sighed, rubbing his eyes. "So, I kept the secret, both out of fear of what she would do, shame over feeling that fear, shame over what had happened. I always felt like I would never have been able to say anything, because how would I prove it?"

"So she showed up at your apartment because she was trying to exert influence? Still?"

Blue nodded. "She's wildly jealous of you, of Magda. We still haven't gotten to the reason why she suddenly dropped her bid for more of Dad's fortune."

Romy stood up and paced, her sorrow now turning to anger. "That fucking bitch." She stopped and turned to Blue. "And I'll bet all the money in the world Gaius knew she was going to do it."

Blue looked surprised. "How?"

"He picked me up that night, outside your apartment. He said he was coming to talk with you. I was so intent in getting away that I didn't question it, but ..."

"Fucker. Conniving motherfucker." Blue was angry now too but Romy put her arms around him.

"Tonight is not the time for retribution. Tonight we're talking, remember. Just you and me."

Blue stared down at her. "I've never told anyone about what Hilary did to me. Not one person. I was stupid to think I could keep it from you, especially after you trusted me enough to tell me about Mortimer."

"There are bad, bad people in the world," Romy said quietly. "And they all have their reasons, however fucked up, to want to hurt us. It's up to us to make sure they can't."

Blue stroked the backs of his fingers down her cheek. "You're right."

Romy leaned into his touch. "Blue ... we're going to get through this, I swear we will." She took his hand and led him to their bedroom. "Let's go to bed, baby. In the morning, we'll talk more, and we'll make a plan where to go from here."

Blue kissed her tenderly. "You got it, beautiful."

IT SEEMED ONLY a few moments after they closed their eyes that the call came, and they knew it was about to be one of the worst days of their lives.

CHAPTER 17

So much blood. The floors of the emergency room were covered with it, making the rushing staff slip and slide in it as they tried to cope with the influx of seriously injured and dying patients.

A high-speed train had missed a stop signal, plowing into another passenger train at the station. Hundreds were injured, dozens dead, and worst of all, as Mac told Romy as they hurriedly changed into scrubs, there were a lot of families.

"There are kids," he said, dead-eyed, and Romy felt sick.

It was worse than she'd expected. Blue, some of his fellow attendings, and Beau Quinto, were all down in the ER or in the operating rooms desperately trying to save people with horrific injuries. The first few hours saw so many people brought in dead that Romy lost count.

The ER was overrun, a warzone, and she yelled out to Mac, "Why aren't the other hospitals taking in emergencies?"

Mac gave a steady look. "They are ..."

"Jesus." Romy could not fathom the scope of the accident. On Christmas night too.

Warren, the orderly she vaguely knew, helped out, arranging

places for the treated to go, and she threw him a grateful glance. "You're the best, Warren."

He nodded shyly. Romy caught sight of Blue, his face pale and stressed. He nodded to her and mouthed, "You okay?"

She nodded. If she let her feelings take over, she would scream.

Beau came over. "Romy, we're sending a team into the field. You, Mac, Blue, and myself will go to begin with. Get some supplies together, as many as we can spare, and let's go."

As THEY RODE in the ambulance down to the King Street Station, Beau briefed them. "The station building itself is undamaged so there's a triage area that has been set up inside. Look, there are a lot of dead and a lot of injured, as you know, but we still have people trapped who might need surgery in situ. It's going to be upsetting and dangerous, but I trust all of you. Stay safe."

Even Beau's words could not have prepared them for the horror of what they found in the mangled wreckage. Romy felt her composure slip when she saw the dead bodies of two children, rendered unrecognizable by their injuries, being lifted from the train, and she turned away, taking in deep breaths. *People need you. Get a grip.*

The doctors went to work with the same efficiency they had employed in their own emergency room. Romy worked closely with the first responders both on the track and in the train's vast waiting area.

Hours passed, night turned into day turned into night again. Drooping from exhaustion, the medical staff nevertheless kept up their treatment, dispatching as many patients as they could to hospitals in the area. The less injured were ferried down as far as Portland to get beds.

Blue came to find Romy as the second night drew on and they grabbed a couple of private moments together.

"You okay, bub?"

She nodded, but she could tell he wasn't convinced. "First major incident?"

She half laughed. "Yep, having a lot of 'firsts' this year."

He hugged her tightly. "Beau says another hour and he'll call it."

"Okay. I'm just going to do another sweep of the place."

"Okay, I'll take the other end of the station. See you in a few."

ROMY CLAMBERED BACK down onto the tracks, careful to avoid the third rail even though they had been assured the power had been switched off. She scooted behind the pile of wreckage and searched around in the dark. Her foot slipped on some blood and she wobbled, falling backwards—but thankfully, was caught by two strong arms.

"Thanks," she said breathlessly, turning to face her savior but before she could see who it was, he grabbed her head and slammed it hard against the steel of the wreckage. Romy didn't even have time to cry out as he attacked her, hitting her head repeatedly against the steel until she was almost unconscious. Blood was pouring from her forehead into her eyes and she could feel herself weakening.

"Hello, my darling," a familiar, horrifying voice growled in her ear as she blacked out. "How ironic that your life should end here, Rome, as you do your Florence Nightingale thing."

No ... no ... it couldn't be, this wasn't how it ended. Romy found she couldn't move her arms to fight him off and as he slipped his hands around her throat, all she could think of was Blue.

God, Blue, I'm sorry, I love you ...

"Romy!"

The pressure on her throat stopped and she heard Dacre's muffled. "Fuck!" Suddenly she knew she was alone and that her would-be killer had gone, but now the darkness was beginning to cloud her vision and the last thing she remembered was Blue's anguished cry.

CHAPTER 18

Beau's handsome face was set and grim as he faced the television cameras. "As you know by now, we have confirmed seventy-eight deaths, one hundred and fifty-three seriously injured, and forty-seven minor injuries in the King Street Station Rail crash. I and my team were on hand to help the first responders, and I would like to thank them for their exceptional service. My team, both with me at the station and here at Rainier Hope, has worked tirelessly for over forty-eight hours since the accident, and I applaud every one of them."

He looked down for a moment, trying to rein in his anger. "Unfortunately, shockingly, during the operation to save the lives of as many victims as possible, one of our doctors, Dr. Romy Sasse, was attacked and seriously injured by an unknown assailant. Dr. Sasse is currently being treated at Rainer Hope for head injuries. We ask anyone who was in the vicinity of the King Street Station on the twenty-sixth of December to come forward with any information they may have." Quinto looked directly into the camera. "Whoever you are, you should know. No one attacks my staff and gets away with it. Whoever you are, you will be brought to justice."

Blue clicked off the television, grateful for his boss's support. In the bed next to him, Romy opened her eyes as she'd been doing intermittently for a while, but this time her eyes focused on him. "Blue?"

He let out a shaky breath. "Thank God ... baby, I was so scared. How do you feel?"

"A little woozy."

"Do you remember what happened?" Blue asked, leaning down to stroke her hair gently.

Romy nodded, then winced.

"Dacre was choking me until he heard you call my name. You saved me, baby."

"I shouldn't have taken my eyes off of you," he said, his eyes sorrowful.

"You can't watch me twenty-four seven, and we had a job to do. Who knew Dacre was psycho enough to do that? Come to think of it ... how the hell did he know I was down there? And why would he risk trying to kill me there with the police all around? He's insane."

"Well, we knew that. Anyway, don't think of that, just get well. That's all I care about right now."

Romy leaned back further into the pillows. "I honestly feel okay, which surprises me. He really did a number on my head."

"They gave you a CT scan before anything. No brain bleeds, thank God, but you'll be concussed for a few days."

Romy pushed the covers on the bed back and swung her legs over the side. Blue was up in an instant.

"Whoa, whoa, whoa. Where are you going?"

"A concussion, I can deal with at home, Blue," Romy said, frowning as he caught her and made her sit again. "I'm taking up a bed when I don't need it."

Blue sighed. "You're not going anywhere, Romy. Beau wanted to keep you in for observation and he's the boss."

"You need the beds for the train victims."

He shook his head. "Honey ... the less seriously injured were taken to hospitals out of the city in anticipation that we would need more beds." His voice was gravelly. "We didn't need as many beds as we hoped we would."

"Oh God," Romy groaned. "How many?"

"Seventy-eight dead, over one-fifty serious, and more than a third of those critical. It was a bad smash, baby."

"Merry fucking Christmas."

"Indeed." He stroked her face and she leaned into his hand. "You might not feel it now because you still have morphine in your system, but honey, you're going to have one hell of a headache when it wears off. So, bed rest. I'm going to be here the whole time."

Romy sighed and got back into bed, reaching up to feel the pattern of butterfly stitches on her head. "Will I at least have some awesome scars?"

Blue chuckled softly. "No, you bled a lot, but the wounds in themselves weren't too serious. The bruising is the main thing."

"Can I see?"

Blue looked at her askance then nodded. He went into the en-suite bathroom to fetch a mirror. "You were one of those kids who bragged when you skinned your knees, right?"

"Hell, yes." She took the mirror from him. "Whoa." Her entire forehead was an angry thundercloud of purple, black, and red, crisscrossed by the white of the stitches. "Yup, this is the look."

"You kind of look like that chick from that film with the road race."

"Penelope Pitstop?"

Blue laughed. "No, the Charlize Theron character from *Mad Max*."

Romy looked impressed. "Furiosa. Yeah, baby." She pulled Blue over to kiss him. "Now that's some roleplay I could get into."

"Ahem."

They both looked up to see a tired-looking but smiling Beau at the door. "Am I interrupting?"

"Not at all." Romy smiled at him. He came into the room, winking at Blue before checking Romy's vitals.

"Good. That's all good."

"So, I can go home?" Romy looked hopeful as Blue rolled his eyes.

Beau grinned. "Not on your life. At least overnight, Dr. Sasse, your chief's orders. Listen," his smile faded and he pulled up a chair, "the police will want to talk to you. I've spoken to the hospital board; we're going to be intensifying the security around here. There will more scrutiny on visitors, on staff. I can't tell you how sorry I am about the attack."

"Thanks, boss."

Beau left them alone a little while later and Blue kissed Romy's hand. "When they let you out, we're going away for a few days. I've cleared it with Beau."

Romy sank back onto the pillows. Her head was beginning to pound painfully now. "Okay." She closed her eyes for a moment, then let out a distressed gasp. "God, Mom. You didn't call her, did you?"

"It was on the news; I had to call Stuart. He told me he would break it to her gently."

"I don't want them coming back and ruining their honeymoon."

Blue stroked her sore head. "I think I persuaded them not to."

"Thank God." Romy leaned into Blue's touch. "I think I need to sleep now."

"You go right ahead. Do you want some painkillers?"

Romy nodded, wincing, and when Blue came back with the tablets, she swallowed them gratefully, draining her water glass. She felt exhausted, drained, and now that the adrenaline had left her system, the shock of the attack was getting to her. She closed her eyes before they could fill with tears and fell into an uneasy sleep.

GAIUS WAS beside himself with rage. "You damn fool! Do you know how many cops were at the accident? You tried and kill her *there*?"

Dacre waited until Gaius had ranted himself out, then narrowed his eyes at the other man. "I didn't intend to *kill* Romy, just scare the crap out of her. I promise you, it worked."

"But you could have been seen; all the work we've done to get you close to her could have been undone."

"You mean like if someone had tried to split them up before we got to finish what we set out to do? Like your slut mother?" Dacre enjoyed the dark rage in Gaius' face.

"Believe me, my mother and I are going to have a serious talk. *God*." Gaius' express was pure disgust. "How could she have slept with that Italian son of a bitch?"

Dacre said nothing, just smirked. Gaius stared at him in dislike. "Yeah. You laugh, but it's Romy's mouth wrapped around his cock now."

Dacre growled and Gaius smirked. "Yeah, that sticks in your craw, doesn't it?"

"Not for much longer."

"Well, this time, stick to what we planned and we'll get everything we ever wanted."

Dacre nodded, but said nothing. Gaius had been useful up to now, but there was no way Dacre would tell him what his real plan was. Something that would make Romy's last moments on Earth a living hell.

CHAPTER 19

After three days, Beau discharged Romy, and Blue immediately whisked her onto his private jet and flew them both to Italy. As she stepped out into the mild Italian winter and felt the sun on her skin, Romy sighed happily. "Yeah, this is what I needed." She smiled at Blue, who was loading their cases into the big hire car. She loved that rich as he was, Blue preferred to do things himself rather than hire a staff.

He drove them through the Tuscan countryside, past olive groves, vineyards and avenues of cypress trees until he pointed out a large villa on top of a hill. "There it is."

Romy saw a terracotta-colored stone villa nestled into the hill and as they approached she sighed. "God, it's beautiful."

"And ours," Blue grinned at her surprise. "Merry Christmas, baby."

Romy gaped at him. "You *bought* this place?"

Blue laughed. "Almost ... I wanted you to have a say, so I'm holding off until you give the final say as to whether I sign the papers. But yeah. I wanted to surprise you."

"You certainly did that."

At the villa, Blue dumped their cases in the lobby. Then, taking

Romy's hand, he walked her through the villa. Exposed brick, billowing white drapes, bookcases, hand-turned wooden furniture—the whole place was a romantic dream. Romy went from room to room, open-mouthed. "God, Blue, I thought these types of places only existed in the movies."

"You like?"

"I *love*."

Blue laughed, delighted. "Good. I'm glad you think so. Come see the kitchen."

The kitchen was a vast open-plan room with an open fire as well as a state-of-the-art stove and range, and a huge wooden table, marked from years of use. Dried herbs hung from the walls, and there were three comfy couches at one end. "This is the heart of the house," Romy said, "you can just tell this is where the people congregate, eat, drink, love. God, can you imagine our family here? Everyone bustling around, Mom taking over the cooking, Juno flopped on the one of the couches."

"Our kids running around." Blue smiled as she looked up at him.

"Someday, hopefully."

He kissed her softly, then as she responded, the kiss became fiercer before he broke away, breathless, studying her. "Do you feel okay?"

Romy nodded. In truth, the injury was still giving her headaches, but she wanted Blue so badly, she pushed aside any doubts. She pressed her body against him. "Take me to bed, Allende."

Blue swept her into his arms and strode through the villa, grinning down at her. "I'm going to kiss every inch of you, pretty girl."

BLUE MADE love to her tenderly, a little hesitantly, conscious that she wasn't fully recovered. The bruises on her lovely face were a daily reminder of how close he had been to losing her and it gnawed away at his gut. Who attacked a doctor at the scene of an accident? Why the hell would Dacre Mortimer risk so much?

Fucker.

When Romy fell asleep, Blue lay awake, his mind whirling with anger and love and confusion. He'd hired the security team—even, here, in Italy, they weren't far away. He hadn't wanted Romy to feel trapped so he'd kept that information to himself, but it reassured him that no one could get to them here. He could relax and Romy could heal.

He eventually fell asleep and was awoken by soft kisses from Romy. He smiled without opening his eyes. "You taste so sweet, baby."

He heard her throaty chuckle, then felt her move down the bed and take his cock into her mouth, running her tongue along the hard shaft and up to the sensitive tip. He gave a soft groan as his cock stiffened and quivered under her touch. He stroked her soft hair as she worked on him, then as he came, she gripped his hips tightly, and he came onto her tongue.

"God, Romy ..."

She climbed up his body and straddled him. Blue opened his eyes and smiled at her. "Good morning, beautiful."

"Morning, handsome. Touch me, Allende."

He grinned at her order and cupped her full breasts in his hands, feeling the pillowy softness of her skin, the small nipples hardening under his touch. "Have I told you how much I love your breasts?"

Romy grinned, her dark hair falling over her shoulders, her makeup-free face ethereal in the early morning light. She guided his cock inside her and Blue sucked in a sharp breath. "And your cunt ... your glorious, silky, tight little cunt ... *Jesus*, Romy ..."

She moved on top of him, taking him in deeper and deeper, clenching her muscles around his cock until he was bucking and shuddering beneath her. As she cried out with her climax, he flipped her onto his back and began to thrust harder and harder, pinning her hands to the bad, holding her gaze as he fucked her.

Romy came again and again and Blue, not able to get enough of her, shivered and shot thick, creamy cum deep into her belly. They collapsed against each other, not caring about morning breath, and kissed passionately. "God, I love you," Blue said, his voice gravelly with emotion.

"I love you, Blue. Let's just keep doing this for the rest of our lives." She was breathless, and Blue admired the way her breasts and bely moved with her breathing. He stroked his hand over the soft curve of her belly.

"You've got a deal," he grinned and kissed her again. She pressed her breasts against his hard chest.

"I've never felt like this, ever," she said in a whisper, touching his face tenderly.

"Probably just the concussion," Blue chuckled, and she laughed.

"No way. This is it for me, Blue. This is real. This is what life is meant to be about."

"I couldn't agree more, Romy Sasse." He wrapped himself around her, looking deep into her eyes. "Marry me. Marry me today, or tomorrow, or however soon we can arrange it."

Romy stared back at him and for a long moment, he thought she might say no. *If she is sensible,* he thought, *she will say no. But God, please, please, Romy, say ...*

"Yes."

For a moment, Blue didn't comprehend her answer then as it sank it, he whooped loudly, overwhelmed, as Romy giggled. He rolled her around on the bed, cheering and laughing until they were both breathless.

After they'd calmed down, he stroked the hair away from her face. "Really?"

"Really."

"God, thank you, thank you, thank you. *Mio Dio, mio Dio.*"

"One condition."

"Yes?"

"We have the ceremony in Italian. It's only fitting."

Blue grinned at her. "I'll coach you on the language."

Romy giggled. "I'll have people check that you haven't made me agree to some kind of sexual deviancy."

"Damn, you caught me." Blue propped himself up on his elbow, grinning down at her. "And I thought you'd like that."

"Oh, I would," Romy laughed. "But you don't have to make me

agree to it, it's implicit." She reached down and stroked his cock, which twitched into life again. "Let's do this, Allende. Make me your wife."

And two days later, that was exactly what he did.

CHAPTER 20

O ctavia Helmond grinned at the message on her phone, and her friend, Mandy, nudged her. "What is it?"

"My sister just got married on a whim in Italy."

"That's romantic. Wait, what sister?" Mandy, who had known Octavia since the beginning of high school, looked confused. "I thought you were an only child."

Octavia grinned and explained her relationship to Romy and the Sasses. "Huh," Mandy said, when Octavia saw a photo of Romy. "She does look like you. Sure she didn't donate eggs seventeen years ago?"

"I think not; she would have been twelve." Octavia rolled her eyes at her friend.

"Her mom could have, though. I'm just saying." They were sitting in the cafeteria of the library, waiting for two of their friends to join them. The new year had brought even more snow and the girls were heading out to do some sledding before retreating to Octavia's house for hot chocolate and pizza.

Rebecca, a fiery redhead, yelled over to them as she entered the café, always one to show off, but good natured, and then quiet but sweet Yelena followed her in. The dark-haired girl had been an emigre from Russian five years ago and before meeting the others, had felt left out and lonely. Octavia had brought her into their fold of tomboys and book nerds and now Yelena was thriving.

They set out in Octavia's four-by-four to go to her father's cabin up in the mountains. Dan hadn't been wild about the idea of four teenage girls alone out there, but Octavia had gently reminded him, they were all adults now.

"Almost," he said, with narrowed eyes but Octavia had stared him down. "Dad."

Dan sighed. "Fine ... but you call me when you get there and text every morning and night."

"Deal."

They reached the cabin after dark and hurriedly brought their luggage inside. Octavia lit the fire and Yelena made some hot chocolate. They sat around chatting and laughing until late, then Octavia stretched her long limbs. "Gonna turn in, I think. Want to be ready for a full-on day tomorrow."

"Hell, yes!" Rebecca raised her mug, cursing as she slopped it all over her. Mandy rolled her eyes and helped her clean it up.

Octavia was the last to fall asleep. She was sharing the room with Mandy, her friend curled up beside her, fast asleep. Octavia snuggled under the covers and closed her eyes.

IT WAS ALMOST dawn when she heard it. A soft cry from the other bedroom woke her. She sat up, listening intently. She heard a strange noise, like a thumping into something soft. What the hell? She swung her legs over the side of the bed and crept out into the hall, moving silently along. As she approached the other room, she began to tremble—something didn't feel right. The door was slightly ajar and to her horror, she saw the hooded figure of a tall man bending over her friends' bed. He was moving his arm up and down and in the moonlight, Octavia saw the glint of steel. Oh god, no ...

For a second she was frozen, not believing what she was seeing then, with nothing else to do, she gave a banshee scream and run to tackle the assailant. She hit him full force but he threw her off easily, sending her crashing back to the wall, banging her head viciously. As she recovered, she heard Mandy running to help.

"No, Mandy, run, get help."

But it was too late. Mandy came crashing through the door, flicking the light on, and then Octavia saw the horror of what had happened. Rebecca and Yelena, both gasping for oxygen, covered in blood, were clutching at the vicious stab wounds in their bellies.

"Oct, Mandy, *run*," Rebecca croaked before the killer shoved the blade into her throat, and she fell back, choking and dying. Octavia scrambled to her feet pushing Mandy back out into the hall, but then there was another masked man, easily picking Mandy up and driving a knife deep into her abdomen so many times, so quickly that Mandy had no chance. The killer dumped her body on the ground and then both of them came after Octavia.

She almost reached the cabin door but then one of them tackled her to the ground, the other grabbing her legs and straddling her. He ripped the top of her pajamas open, then to Octavia's disbelief, he pulled his mask off.

Gaius. He grinned down at her. "Well, now, I guess I'm quite the surprise."

"Please don't kill me, Gaius, please."

He laughed, looking at the other assailant. "Well, it's always worth asking, isn't it?" He slowly pushed the knife into her navel and Octavia gasped at the horrific pain. Gaius buried the knife into her to the hilt.

"I did some research, little Octavia, some digging around in the files of the surrogacy place. Seems like we're related. Magda Sasse *is* your biological mother, which makes you Romy's sister—which means we're going to kill you the same way we're going to kill her. Slowly. Painfully. Without mercy." He wrenched the knife from her and Octavia could feel her blood pumping from the wound. Gaius smiled.

"Ah, damn ... I think I've gone and severed your abdominal artery.

You'll bleed out in a few minutes, so we'd better make the most of this …"

Octavia screamed as the other killer drew his own knife out of his pocket and both men stabbed her again and again until there was nothing left but darkness.

CHAPTER 21

Romy Sasse-Allende rolled over in bed and smiled at her husband. "Hey, hubby."

Blue opened his eyes and grinned. "Hey, wifey." He leaned over to kiss her and she wriggled into his arms, hooking a leg over his body. She could feel his cock stiffening as she pressed her body against him.

"Fuck me, husband."

With a chuckle, Blue rolled her onto her back, and hitched her legs around his waist. "Damn, you're so wet."

Romy grinned up at him sleepily. "I've been dreaming about you." She moved her body so her breasts and belly undulated and with a growl, Blue plunged his cock deep inside her ready and swollen cunt, pining her hands to the bed, and thrusting with measured but brutal strokes into her. Romy moaned and encouraged him as he fucked her, loving it when he got rough, coming over and over as he shot his load inside of her. He flipped her onto her stomach and eased into her ass, pulling her hair as she screamed his name.

They tore and clawed at each other, the bed moving with the violence of their lovemaking. Blue fucked her against the wall of the shower, lifting her easily in his strong arms, Romy bracing herself against the cool tile as his cock reamed her cunt until she thought she might not be able to take it anymore.

As they made breakfast, he bent her over the counter and took her from behind, telling her over and over how much he loved her, then later, as they walked in the olive groves, he had her again, staking his claim of her body as well as her heart, fucking intensely until they were both breathless and sated.

Evening was falling as they made their way back towards the villa. Blue was picking grass and twigs from her long dark curls, and his eyes were so soft with love, that Romy couldn't help but stop to kiss him. He ran his hands down her body.

"How did I ever exist before you, Romy Sasse?"

Romy grinned up at him. "Romy Sasse Allende. And I don't know, Blue, because there was nothing before you."

He grinned. "I think we just exceeded our cheese quote for the year."

Romy laughed. "I don't care. This is our honeymoon, gorgeous man; cheesy is a requirement. You know what's also a requirement?"

"What?"

"Food. I'm *starving*."

Blue drove them into Florence to a favorite restaurant of his, and they dined on lobster and pasta and garlic bread, moaning over the delicious food. Blue ordered some wine and they lingered over desserts of Zabaglione with fresh berries.

The coffee was strong and dark, and they sat talking long into the evening. Romy leaned her head on Blue's shoulder. "I'm so chilled right now. This place is heavenly."

"I'm glad you think so. So, what's the verdict? Should I close on the villa?"

Romy nodded, smiling. "Blue, we haven't discussed kids, but I think the villa would be the perfect place to bring them up."

He smiled warmly. "I do too, baby."

Across the street was a row of stores, each different, none of them brand names, all family owned, some of them still open this late in the evening. There was something so pure and natural about this place, Romy thought. Her eye was caught by the flickering of a television in the bar across the street. For a moment, she couldn't believe what she was seeing.

"Tavia?" No, it couldn't be. Her young friend's face flashed up again, and Romy saw now that the news channel was focusing on a snowbound crime scene, police tape fluttering around a small log cabin. Romy stood up to move closer to the television and Blue, hurriedly throwing a wad of Euros down to pay for their meal, followed her.

They had been cut off from cell phone and Internet access for a few days and both had enjoyed it, but now, Romy stared in horror at the television. "Can you turn that up, please?" she asked anyone who would listen.

Blue repeated the question in Italian and the bartender grabbed the remote and increased the volume.

The four young women, all aged seventeen, were found stabbed to death this morning by the owner of this isolated log cabin. It is believed he is also one of the girl's father, local businessman Daniel Helmond.

"No!" Romy's legs gave way as Blue dived to catch her. "No, no, no, not Tavia, please, *please, not Tavia.*" She was screaming, not caring that the entire street was staring at her.

THE VICTIMS HAVE NOW BEEN OFFICIALLY IDENTIFIED as *Rebecca Moore, Octavia Helmond, Mandy Fitkins, and Yelena Shostakovich. All the women were from Kings County, Seattle; all were brutal stabbed to death. Police say the killer or killers left very little physical evidence of themselves and have asked that anyone with any information come forward. Back to the studio.*

TWO HOURS LATER, when Romy had finally gotten through to a devastated Artemis, she spoke with her sister for a few minutes then came back to the table. She was calm now, too calm, Blue thought as he stood to take her in his arms. The restaurant was officially closed but the owner was a kindly man who told them to take all the time they needed to make calls. He kept them supplied with hot, strong coffee, and pastries although neither Blue or Romy could eat.

Romy leaned against her new husband's body. "We have to go back. It's Dacre. He'll keep killing innocent women. We have to draw him out."

"Romy ..."

"No, Blue. No objections. It's the only thing left to do." She looked up into his eyes and he could see the endless sorrow in them. "I won't go down without a fight. And I'll play dirty, Blue, believe me."

"You're not in this alone."

"I know." She sighed, squeezing her eyes shut to stop them from tearing up again. She felt raw from screaming. "For tonight, let's go home."

"I'll book the plane for tomorrow."

"Thank you, baby."

DACRE AND GAIUS watched the news with satisfaction, then Gaius grabbed a couple of beers from his fridge. Dacre clinked his bottle against Gaius' and then sat back, studying the other man.

"How did it feel? Your first kill?"

Gaius smiled. "Godlike."

Dacre laughed. "I'll drink to that." He took a long swig. "Romy will be on her way back to the states now."

"So her sister says."

Dacre sighed. "It's time, man. When we were killing those girls, all I could think of was doing the same thing to Romy. Sticking that knife into her gut over and over. I got hard just thinking about it."

Gaius nodded. "I agree, it's time."

Dacre was deep in thought. "The best place to do it will be at the hospital. No one suspects me there; hell, she doesn't even recognize me."

"Well, you did do a transformation from preppy asshole to

redneck psycho." Gaius smiled as Dacre laughed. "Yeah, she won't see you coming."

"God," Dacre grabbed his cock and squeezed it. "The anticipation of that pop, the moment when my knife cuts into her skin."

"Dude, don't jerk off in front of me." Gaius' nose was turned up in disgust, but Dacre just laughed.

"Don't flatter yourself, asshole." He took another long drink of beer. "So, what about you? You gonna fuck your brother up? Or are you going to leave him alone to mourn Romy?"

"Both." Gaius' eyes glittered with malice. "I'm going to beat him to within an inch of his life, then drag him to watch you kill Romy. How does that sound?"

Dacre's smile spread slowly across his face. "Dude ... that sounds just about perfect."

The funeral was well-attended and as painful as they all expected. Octavia's coffin was lowered into the cold January ground; Dan, her father, had such a look of desolation on his face that Romy could barely look at him. The guilt she felt was overwhelming, and since she and Blue had flown back to Seattle, a week ago, she had been working with the police to try and smoke Dacre out.

At the hospital, she and Blue had had a conference with Beau and the head of security and decided the measures would stay for now. "I'm not risking your life or anyone else's, Romy." Beau said. "I've had experience at the vengeful ex thing—my Dinah nearly died."

"I know, Beau, and thank you." Romy looked between the two men. "I'm so sorry for bringing this all down on your heads."

"It's not your fault," Blue repeated for what seemed the hundredth time, but Romy couldn't help but feel it pressing down on her. Octavia's horrific murder had affected the whole family —Dan, to his credit, hadn't blamed her, or Artemis but Romy almost wanted him to yell and scream at her.

At night, after she and Blue were in bed, after her adored husband was asleep, his arms tight around her, Romy would lie awake, thinking up ways to bait Dacre into revealing himself, and then coming up with increasing violent ways to kill him herself. Her rage was all-consuming. She would sleep for a couple of hours then get up, grab her laptop, and go through all the information she could find on Dacre, his family, the murders. On more than one morning, Blue had found her asleep on the couch, her laptop still open.

She knew Blue was worried about her and couldn't blame him for being so. Never, even after the attack of the previous year, had she felt so on edge, like she was on a tightrope and nothing could stop her from falling.

Only at work could she focus on what she was doing. She and Blue were even more in tune in the operating theater, and even their recent marriage hadn't affected her relationship with her colleagues —much to her relief.

Mac was the only other resident who knew everything. Romy found she was leaning on him more and more, someone outside their family, a friend, a sounding post. She had told him —then told him to forget it.

"Everything I talk about now seems to be about Dacre," she said, with a sad smile. "Promise me that when we talk, we'll bust each other's chops or just talk about work, or our love lives—rather, your love life."

Mac smiled, his smile splitting his handsome face and lighting it up. "You got it, gorgeous."

And he kept his word, joking with her, relieving some of that stress. Romy had never been so grateful to someone as she was to Mac.

MAGDA, back from her honeymoon, was stressed out and hyper when Romy went over to her house to visit. After Magda had hugged her for way too long, Romy escaped her mother's arms and rolled her eyes. "Mom, I'm fine. It's Arti and Dan you should be worried about."

"Oh, I am," Magda said, grim-faced, "but Dacre's not trying to kill them, is he?" She sighed and covered her face and, to her distress, Romy saw her mother was crying. She went to her.

"Mom, I have protection coming out of my ears. Look at the two hulking guys I had to bring with me to come visit. Dacre's not going to get to me unless I let him."

Magda dropped her hands and glared at her daughter. "What does that mean? Unless you let him?"

Romy silently cursed herself for the slip. "Just a figure of speech, Mom, chill out."

Magda sighed, her usually youthful face seeming older.

"When you were in the hospital last year," Magda said, "I sat with you, and in my head, I was making up ways I could kill Dacre Mortimer. Some pretty hardcore things."

Romy half-smiled. "You and me both, Mom."

Magda nodded, hesitated, then fixed Romy with a steady look. "Could you? Could you do it? Kill him?"

Romy, grim-faced nodded. "I wouldn't even hesitate."

Magda nodded. "Good. God, Romy, I hate that I couldn't protect you then and can't protect you now."

"What are you talking about? You gave me and Arti and Junebug the best childhood ever. Ever, Mom. The love in this house, that was all down to you. That we've all followed out dreams, that's all because of you. You are my superhero, Mom."

Magda was openly crying now and Romy wrapped her arms around her mother. "Mom, we will get through this."

Magda nodded. She looked at Romy. "Darling, there's something I have to tell you."

Romy, trying to lighten the mood, smiled at her. "Did Stuart knock you up?" She regretted the joke immediately when she saw her mother wince. "God, Mom, what is it?"

"Darling, come sit down. This isn't going to be easy."

. . .

LATER THAT NIGHT, Blue came home to find Romy sitting in the dark. He knew at once that something had happened and he sat down beside her. "What is it?"

Romy looked at him and the sorrow in her eyes was bottomless and searing. "Octavia was my sister. The police told Artemis and Dad that she matched Mom's DNA. Mom told me that twenty years ago she donated her eggs after she'd had Juno. She knew she was done, so she and Dad had eggs fertilized and donated. That's why Tavia looked just like me. We *were* sisters."

"God, no." Blue felt the shock reverberating through his body. Romy looked at him, eerily calm.

"This ends now, Blue. No more. If it kills me, Dacre Mortimer is going down."

Blue looked at his wife unhappily. "This won't end well, Romy."

"I know, baby, but we will prevail. We will be ready."

Romy had no idea how soon she would have to put her theory into practice.

CHAPTER 23

Beau wasn't happy, but eventually he agreed to Romy's request that her protection at the hospital be removed. "At least the visible protection," Blue amended, with a glance at his wife. "Romy's determined to draw him out."

"He knows I'm in Seattle; he knows I work here." Romy looked at Blue. "Blue's arranged for a journalist to interview me about the murders. I'm going to goad him in the press so that he has no option but to come after me."

Beau exchanged a look with Blue and Romy sighed. "Fellas, it's up to me. I'm the one he wants, and I won't let anyone dictate my life."

Later, she was working in the resident's lounge when Warren, the friendly orderly, knocked on the door. "Hey, Dr. Sasse, can I run something past you?"

Romy smiled at him. "Go for it."

Warren came in and sat down. "Staff's been talking. About what's going on with you and this jerk ex of yours."

Romy felt a little awkward. "People are talking."

"Yeah ... sorry if that's inappropriate, but we look after our own around here."

Romy smiled at him. "That's sweet, but I think we got it handled."

"I'm just saying … I'm around. You ever feel threatened, I got your back."

Romy was moved. "Warren, you're the best, but I think I got this. I can be pretty badass."

Warren laughed. "I have no doubt. Well, I said what I wanted to, so …"

"Thanks, Warren. I do appreciate it."

After the orderly had gone, Romy felt strange, like somehow her friends and colleagues were looking at her as if she were a victim. God, that was the last thing she needed. Her stomach roiled and she pushed away from the table and got up, determined to stop feeling sorry for herself.

The hospital was quiet now as the day ended and Romy checked the surgical schedule, seeing that Blue was still operating on an elderly woman with appendicitis. She checked on all of their post-surgical patients and set out about updating the medical records.

She'd just glanced at the clock and seen it was nearly two a.m., when she heard the first shot. Freezing, for a moment she wondered if it was a car backfiring in the lot, then when she heard the screams starting Romy began to run towards the sound of the shooting, joined quickly by other staff and the hospital's security team.

More gunfire and security stopped the medical staff. "Shooting's coming from the OR floor."

Romy's heart nearly failed and she darted forward only to be stopped by one of the security guards. "Sorry, Doc, we can't let you go down there."

"But Blue is there," Rom said, her voice rising as the panic set in.

Mac grabbed her upper arm. "Romy, come on. We need to take care of our patients. Let the security team do their job."

"Hospital is on lockdown," the security chief was telling them all, "go back to where you were and secure your patients as best you can."

Mac dragged Romy back to the post-surgical patients. Some of them were awake now, wondering what was going on. Romy tried to reassure them but when the gunfire came closer, there was a palpable sense of panic.

"Let's get the patients who can't walk and can't hide into secure rooms," Mac said and Romy nodded, her stomach roiling with panic. She grabbed her cell phone and texted Blue.

Are you safe?

There was no answer. When she saw the head of security again, she grabbed him. "What's going on?"

"Shooter." He looked at her as if she was stupid and Romy rolled her eyes.

"I know that ... where is he or she? Is anyone hurt?"

"I don't know, Doc. It's a developing situation."

He moved away before she had a chance to ask any more questions and she hissed in frustration. She tried to call Blue, but knowing he switched off his cell phone when he was in surgery, prayed that was the reason he wasn't answering.

Please, please, be okay.

God, how much more horror would they have to put up with? Romy did her job, helped patients, made sure the floor was secure, but she couldn't help wondering how the hell a man with a gun got into the hospital. Was it because Beau had reduced the security at her request?

Don't be stupid—this has nothing to do with you.

But her instincts were telling her otherwise. Romy felt her composure slip, and she darted into an empty room and dragged some deep breaths into her lungs. *He's fine, he's okay.*

There was a soft knock on the door. "Yes?"

Warren opened the door and gave her a hesitant smile. "You okay, Doc?"

She shook her head. "No. There's a shooter down on the OR floor and Blue is there. No, I'm not okay, Warren. They won't let me go to him."

He stared at her for a long moment, then said, "I can get you down there."

Romy's eyes widened. "You can?"

Warren nodded, his eyes watchful as he gazed at her. "I can. Come with me."

Romy didn't even think twice, such was her need to get to Blue. She followed Warren into the far end of the floor, raising her eyebrows as he opened the fire escape.

"No alarm."

"No, they shut the power down on the doors to contain the shooter, which knocked out the alarms. But this door has always been tricky."

She followed him down two flights of stairs then as he passed the OR floor, she faltered. "Warren?"

He turned and grabbed her hand, pulling her after him. "We have to go down to go up, Rome."

It took a second to process what he'd called her and a wave of utter horror swept over her. "What did you call me?"

Warren's hand tightened on her wrist as he turned back towards her. "Miss me, Rome?"

It couldn't be ... Romy stared at the big man in horror, and began to see it. Dacre had completely changed his body type; his hair was gone; the thick beard; the piercings ... but yes, it was her ex-husband.

"How did I not see it?" she said out loud and as Dacre pulled her into his grip, he laughed.

"Because you didn't want to. You've only had eyes for the Italian, haven't you, whore? His hands all over you?"

He was dragging her down the stairs, her petite body no match for his strength. "They'll find your body in the basement, Rome, gutted, bled out. Of course, by that time I'll be long gone. They'll still be looking for whoever is shooting up the hospital."

"Motherfucker, that was you? Killing more innocent people?"

"Dumb bitch, there is no shooter. The dumb security team is going through the hospital trying to find someone who isn't there. I set it up so someone would fire blanks nearby and panic everybody."

Confused by his certainty, Romy was trying desperately to put her hand in her pocket. She had a hypodermic needle in there—if she could just reach it, she could use it as a weapon ... her fingers closed around it and with all her might, she gripped it in her fist and plunged it backwards, aiming for Dacre's face. She felt resistance then, as Dacre howled and released her, she knew she'd hit her mark. Dacre jerked back, the needle piercing his left eye. "Fucking bitch!"

Romy didn't wait around. He was blocking the way upwards, so she went down, practically flying down the staircase. In her pocket, her cell phone began to buzz. *Blue.*

"Baby, where are you? The freakiest thing, there's some kind of ..."

"Blue! It's Dacre ... he's here, he's after me... I'm in staircase C and I don't know where I can get away from him."

"God, baby, go down as far as you can, to the basement, you can get to the foyer. From there I ..."

There was a scuffling noise and she heard Blue cry out in anger and pain and Romy screamed. "Blue!"

"Romy ..." And then the phone went dead. What the hell was going on? Behind her, she heard Dacre crashing down the stairs after her. What the hell had happened to Blue?

She pushed her way into the basement of the hospital, a vast labyrinth of pipes and dank corridors. Romy ran as fast as she could, towards what she thought was the front of the hospital. Dacre was almost on her as she flung the door open and ran out into the foyer of the hospital.

Dacre grabbed her and they both tumbled to the floor, Romy struggling with his vast weight on top of her. Even a glimpse at the blade of the knife he pulled out made her mad rather than scared and she kicked and bit and clawed at him as he tried to subdue her.

"No," she screamed at him, "You don't get to win this time, Dacre. Never again."

He laughed at her, cuffing her viciously around the face. "Give it up, bitch; it was always going to end this way."

He was winning, his sheer physical size overpowering her. He bounced Romy's head off the cold hard floor and as she reeled, he pinned her. His mouth ground down on hers, his tongue penetrating her mouth. Romy bit down on it as hard as she could, tasting blood, and Dacre roared in pain and anger.

He drew back his arm, ready to stab her, but then everything stopped. Dacre's eyes widened suddenly as blood began to pour from his chest. Romy whimpered as he fell forward onto her, then kicked him off of her, her eyes whirling wildly around the room.

Behind them, Gaius Eames lowered the gun he was holding. Romy hadn't even heard the shot.

"Gaius!"

He came to her immediately, helping her to her feet, his expression incredulous. "Are you all right? Are you hurt? Who the fuck was that?"

Romy leaned against him, relieved to find a friendly face even if it was Gaius. "My ex-husband. And no, I'm not hurt."

"Good." He pressed his lips to her temple, wrapping his arm around her, and Romy felt comforted.

"Blue. I have to get to Blue."

Gaius nodded and tucked his gun in his pants. Romy blinked. "Gaius, why do you have a gun?"

"I have a permit to carry a concealed weapon," he said, shrugging. He nodded at Dacre's body. "Thankfully."

"Amen to that, but you might want to be careful. He set it up so it sounded like someone was shooting up the place, and if security sees you with a weapon ..."

Gaius nodded. "Yeah, let's get out of here. Find Blue and get out."

They made their way carefully to the OR floor. It was dark, silent, and Romy felt a coldness settle over her. She could smell cordite in the air. OR3. That was where Blue had been operating. She led Gaius towards it, the smell of gunsmoke stronger.

Romy pushed her way into the scrub room and looked through the window. The OR was a mess, blood, instruments, drapes everywhere. She pushed into the room—and saw him.

He was covered in blood and Romy screamed, dropping to her knees by his side. "Blue?"

He opened his eyes, the bright green stark against the blood on his face. He smiled. "You're here."

"Are you shot?" Romy was running her hands over his body, trying to find wounds. Blue shook his head.

"No, he only hit me. God, Romy, I never knew. I never knew he hated me that much."

Ice flooded through her veins. "Dacre didn't even know you, Blue; he just wanted you out of the way."

Blue looked confused. "No, not Dacre, Romy ..." He trailed off as he looked behind her and his face went pale. "Romy ..."

Romy whirled around to find Gaius, smiling at them both, and aiming the gun at Blue. "No, Romy, Dacre didn't know much about Blue. He wanted to kill you, beautiful, and I offered to help—as long as Blue was made to witness your murder. Then, well, Dacre became a loose end. After we killed your ... what was she ... sister? Octavia, anyhow, and her friends, I knew I wanted to do you myself, but Dacre wouldn't hear of it. So he had to go."

Romy was staring at him aghast, then with a scream, she threw herself at Gaius. He had anticipated it and easily threw her off, but not before Blue had a chance to scramble to his feet and go after his half-brother.

"You bastard! *Figlia di puttana!*"

Gaius was a big man but nothing to Blue's strength. The two men crashed to the floor and Romy cast around desperately for something to help Blue. She grabbed a scalpel and leapt at Gaius, slashing at him. She caught his arm and he yelled as Blue landed a punch so hard that Gaius fell backward. As he scrambled away from them, he pulled out his gun.

Blue stopped as Gaius aimed it at him. "Gaius, don't be stupid. Killing me won't help you. This place is crawling with cops. They'll cut you down in an instant."

Gaius stared at him as Blue and Romy, holding their breaths, stood still. Then Gaius's mouth hitched up in a smile. "You're right." And he swung his arm and shot Romy.

The bullet smashed into her belly and she dropped as Blue, half-crazed with grief, went for Gaius. Gaius was too quick for him, putting the gun to his own temple. "You fucked my mom," he said, sounding like a child.

Blue shook his head. "She raped me, Gaius."

"No."

Blue, seeing the half-crazed expression in Gaius' eyes, but desperate to get to Romy, crouched next to his half-brother. "Don't do it, Gaius. Your mom is a bad person, but she loves you."

Gaius half-smiled. "She's nothing anymore. I strangled her to death the day after I found out she fucked you. They've probably found her body by now."

Blue was horrified. "Jesus, Gaius."

Gaius was staring at Romy now, who was clutching at her bleeding stomach, but calmly, deeply breathing, watching the scene play. "She's lovely, Blue. So lovely. I'm glad I got to kill her before I died." And he put the gun in his own mouth and pulled the trigger.

Blue didn't hesitate. He went to Romy and gathered her into his arms. Romy stared up at him, still unnaturally calm. "Blue," she said in a steady voice, "Blue ... save our baby. Please, save our little one. I love you so much." Her eyes closed and she passed out.

Shell-shocked, Blue swept her out of the room and into an unused OR. Keeping his hand pressed to the bullet wound, he grabbed his phone. "Beau, the shooter is dead. But Romy's been shot. I need a team in OR2 right now. Please, help me save my girl ... and our child. Please ..." His voice shook, but he knew that to lose control now was to sentence Romy to death. "Please, Beau ... I need you right now ..."

CHAPTER 24

Romy opened her eyes and wondered why she felt no pain. *It's the morphine, doofus.* She breathed in a lungful of sweet pure air and smiled. Looking around the room, she saw Blue checking her chart. He glanced up and grinned. "Hey, beautiful."

"Get over here and kiss me, Allende."

"Such a nag." But he pressed his lips to hers and they kissed until they had to break away to breathe. He stroked her cheek. "How do you feel?"

"Good, really good. Blue ... how's ...?"

"Our baby? He or she is doing just fine. How come you didn't tell me?"

"I was going to, but I hadn't even taken a test yet." Romy sighed, putting her hand on her belly. "I can't be more than a couple of weeks; I just had a feeling."

"Three weeks to be precise," Blue grinned, covering her hand with his. "I can't wait to meet him or her."

"We're really going to do this, right?" Romy felt nervous and excited and Blue laughed.

"You bet your sweet ass we are. We got married on a rollercoaster ride; we're gonna start our family the same way. You in this adventure with me?"

Romy gazed up at her husband and grinned. "Just try and stop me."

THREE MONTHS LATER...

BLUE SMILED at his excited wife. "I honestly thought you'd fight me on this."

"Are you kidding? This is our honeymoon, Blue. We earned this."

They were flying in Blue's private jet down to the Caribbean, and to one of the lesser-known islands, owned by a friend of Blue's.

Romy had recovered quickly from the shooting and now, their child growing in her belly, she was ready to return to work. Blue, however, had insisted on them taking some time together first, and so for the next two blissful weeks, they would make love, laze in the sun, eat whatever they wanted.

"I cannot wait," Romy stretched out her body and rubbed Blue's groin with her foot, "to get naked and rude with you, Blue boy."

Blue laughed and went to her. "Why wait?" He pulled her gently to the cabin floor and kissed her until they were both breathless. Romy tangled her fingers in his dark curls as he unbuttoned her dress, parting the fabric and pressing his mouth to her soft skin. Blue freed her breasts from her bra, taking each nipple into his mouth in turn and teasing them into hard peaks. Romy sighed happily as he moved down her body, kissing the soft swell of her belly as he gently slid the panties down her legs.

"I want you inside me," she whispered and grinning, Blue moved to kiss her mouth as he freed his cock from his pants.

"You want me inside, pretty girl?"

Romy giggled, seeing the mischievous lust in his eyes. "Always ... *Oh!*"

Blue thrust his cock deep inside her, pinning her hands above her head and kissing her with animal passion. Romy hitched her legs around his waist, tilting her hips up to take him in deeper. Nothing else in the world existed for them as they made love, their gazes locked, their bodies perfectly in rhythm.

As she came, Romy's back arched up and Blue buried his face in her neck as he shot his seed into her. They collapsed together, panting for air and laughing. Blue kissed her and Romy stroked his face. "I love you so much, Blue Allende."

"You and me forever, baby."

Romy grinned and squeezed his butt playfully as she nodded. "You bet your sweet ass, gorgeous man."

And they made love again as the plane came in to land in their Caribbean paradise ...

The End.

Did you like this book? Then you'll LOVE Her Dark Melody.

On the worst day of my life, she was there...
Ebony...her voice enchanted me, her beauty made me breathless.
When she sang for me and my twin brother Mateo at our Halloween party, I knew I had to make her mine.
I wanted her in my life, my arms, my bed...
Nothing could stop how we felt about each other, nothing...
But then a terrible tragedy struck and suddenly life came to a halt.
Ebony is the only reason I carry on now, the only reason I breathe in and out.
When we make love, it's the only time I can feel happiness...
But someone wants to take her away from me.
I can't let it happen, can't let my beautiful girl be ripped away from me.
She's all I have left...

Start reading Her Dark Melody: A Christmas Romance (Season of Desire 3) NOW!

THE NAUGHTY ONE EXTENDED
EPILOGUE

Five years after they met and fell in love, Romy Sasse and Blue Allende are both loving parents to Grace, and at the top of their game in the surgical world. As Blue is named as Chief of Surgery at Rainier Hope Hospital, Romy is courted by another hospital, eager to have her come on board with them as their own Head of General Surgery. Romy has to make the decision whether she wants to stay working under her husband and suffer career setbacks because of internal politics, or take the job, work away from her family and possibly risk her marriage.
With only a week to decide over Christmas, Romy, Blue and Grace head for their mountain hideaway to enjoy the holidays together, and Romy comes to a decision which will change all of their lives forever...

≈

B lue lifted his four-year old daughter onto his shoulders, grinning as Grace giggled, clutching onto her father's dark curls. "You okay up there, slugger?"

"Yes, Papa."

Romy smiled at them both. Grace looked so much like her father, all bright green eyes and dark brown curls, though Grace's were long and wild, and Blue's were shot through with silver now. Romy marveled at her beautiful family, at the two people who meant the most to her in the world. "You ready, kids?"

Both Blue and Grace laughed. "Let's do it."

The SUV was loaded with their bags, and boxes full of gifts, mostly for Grace. Blue strapped his daughter securely into her car seat as Romy climbed into the driver's seat and set up the Sat-Nav. They'd bought the lodge in the Olympic Mountains only this year and Romy still wasn't sure of the way. In fact, she'd only seen photographs on the realtor's website – Blue had been the one to visit it and give the final verdict.

She still remembered when he'd come home the night he'd viewed it, shining eyes and enthusiasm making him seem manic. "It's perfect, Romy, just perfect."

"Is it cozy?"

He'd hesitated and Romy had grinned. She knew the lodge was beyond what most people would dream of, all carved wood furniture and fittings, huge picture windows, a state of the art kitchen as well as huge bedrooms. "*We'll* make it cozy." Blue promised and Romy hadn't doubted it.

Now as they began the long drive from Seattle, Romy was both excited and nervous. Excited for Christmas with her loves, but also nervous about the decision she had to make.

Since their Chief of Surgery Beau Quinto had resigned from his position to move away from Seattle, Blue had been Beau's first and only choice to replace him. Romy was thrilled for her husband – Blue had worked tirelessly and with utmost loyalty for Beau and Rainier Hope, and he deserved every bit of his success.

It was only after they'd really thought about the implications of his new job that reality had hit. Romy was the best Attending the hospital had, but she was also his wife. To others, it might look as if Blue was favoring her if he promoted her, and Romy was worried her own reputation could suffer. On the other hand, she was one of the best, and so if Blue didn't promote her out of fear of impropriety, Romy's career would suffer.

"I'll tell Beau no," Blue had declared, determined. "There's no way I would ever put my career above yours, baby. No way."

Romy smiled at him, moved. "You will *not* tell Beau no. We'll find another way, but I'm not letting you hold yourself back for me. You earned this, Blue, you paid for it with your blood. You *are* the Chief of Surgery."

It took her a few weeks to persuade him but finally, Blue had acquiesced. Then, two weeks later, Romy got a phone call from Portland General.

We want you to be our new Head of General. We won't be the first or last to headhunt you, Dr. Sasse, your reputation precedes you.

Portland. Yes, it was only three hours away by car, but that meant six hours traveling time a day – or she could fly, which meant two of three hours traveling. And that was on the days when she wasn't delayed by surgeries or emergencies or just by the workload of a Chief Attending. The excitement she'd felt after their phone call and offer dissipated quickly. It would mean barely seeing Blue and Grace, never being there for bedtimes or bath-times or after school plays. *God.*

Portland had been right. More offers came in thick and fast but she dismissed them all – except Portland. Now they had given her until New Year's Eve to decide.

Blue had been her champion, and they talked about it one night, after Grace was asleep. Romy lay in his arms, her naked body pressed against his. Blue kissed her tenderly. "You deserve this, baby. Look, I'll do the commute. We'll move home, go to Portland. We both love it there, anyway, so it won't be a wrench."

"But then the exact problems I face will be yours. And you're the Chief, dude. Beau was a workaholic and so are you." Romy had sighed. "And I *love* our home. And I don't want Gracie in the hands of childminders all the time. I want to be able to pick her up from school, play with her, help her with her homework."

Blue grinned. "Yep, she needs all the help she can get with trig at age five."

Romy laughed. "The younger she starts...but seriously, no. Look, there are other things I can explore...maybe even going out on my own."

"Private practice?"

Romy nodded. "But not elitist. Something where anyone could come and be treated, regardless of financial restrictions."

"So, a free clinic?"

"Yeah...but I haven't thought it all through yet so, in the meantime..."

Blue stroked her face. "Whatever you decide, we'll make it work." He suddenly grinned. "Have you ever used trig at work?"

"Never. Not once in my whole adult life."

Blue kissed her, running his hands down her body. "The only 'triangle' I'm interested in right now is *this* one." And he slipped his hand between her legs as Romy wriggled with pleasure. "Well, doc, I may need to find out the angle here, but, oh no, it seems to be widening..."

Romy was giggling, tears in her eyes. "No, Allende, you can't make trig sexy, no way...*oh!*"

Blue thrust his diamond-hard cock into her and they made love slowly, leisurely until they were both exhausted. Blue fell asleep in her arms, but Romy lay awake thinking. *What do I want from my life? Do I really have to choose this, my family, or my career? Why can't I have it both ways?*

She'd fallen asleep without making a decision and now, as they drove through a snowy Washington State, she wanted nothing more than to just relax and enjoy this time away with her family.

BLUE HAD ARRANGED for the lodge's fires to be lit and the huge kitchen supplied with everything they needed for their vacation. The windows glowed with warm welcome as they finally reached the lodge after dark. Grace, asleep for most of the journey, was eager to be let out to play in the thick blanket of snow that surrounded the home. Romy freed her daughter from her restraints and held her hand as Grace yelped with joy and threw herself into the snow.

"Little lunatic." Romy said fondly, then shrieked as Blue dumped a snowball down her back. The three of them then spent twenty minutes play-fighting, before Romy ordered them indoors to get dry and warm.

After a supper of hot steak sandwiches and fully loaded baked potatoes, they sat in front of the fire in the living room, cuddled together on the huge, comfortable couch.

"Tomorrow, we'll decorate the tree," Blue told Grace, nodding to the bare spruce tree in the corner of the room. Grace smiled.

"Lots of twinkle lights?"

"Of course, Boo."

Blue wrapped his arms around his girls, meeting Romy's gaze. He pressed his lips to hers and nuzzled her neck. "Later," he murmured in her ear and Romy knew exactly what he meant. Her heart beat faster – still, after all these years, he could do that to her – and she smiled, her eyes lazy with lust.

"Later."

Grace was overexcited and stayed up way after her usual bedtime, but Romy shrugged. "It's Christmas."

Finally, just after midnight, Romy crept out of Grace's room and closed the door. She padded quietly downstairs to see that Blue had switched off the overhead lights and draped strings of tiny white lights around the room. He'd dragged the sofa back and laid a comforter on the floor in front of the fire. Romy smiled at him as he offered her his hand and pulled her gently into his arms.

The moment his lips met hers, Romy closed her eyes, feeling any tension leave her body. They kissed for a long time, Blue's fingers stroking her face as she pressed her own hands on the hard planes of his chest.

"God, I love you, Romy Sasse."

"I love you too, Blue Allende."

His fingers were at the buttons on her dress now, and as he gently undressed her, he kissed her exposed skin, making her shiver with desire. She pulled his sweater over his head, making his hair even messier, then freed his cock, so thick, hard and long, from his pants.

She stroked the length of it, feeling it twitch and harden in her hands.

Blue stroked her clit until it was hard, then slid two fingers inside her. "You're so wet, baby."

"For you, always."

He swept her onto the floor, kissing her mouth. Romy lay under him, enjoying the weight of his body on hers, feeling the tip of his cock nudging at her sex, then as it notched into her cunt, Blue thrust his hips hard and sank deep inside her.

"God, that feels so good," Romy moaned as he moved slowly in and out of her, never taking his eyes off hers. Romy tightened her thighs around his hips. "Fuck me *hard*, Allende."

Blue grinned, increasing his pace, as Romy dug her fingernails into his buttocks. "*Mio Dio,* you're so goddamn sexy, baby...I'm going to fuck you all night long, ream your silky cunt until you beg me to stop..."

"I'll *never* beg you to *stop*," Romy said, breathlessly, her breasts moving, her nipples brushing his chest as they fucked. "Take me, Blue, take me like you want to hurt me..."

Blue gave a growl and pinned her hands to the floor, slamming his hips against hers, his cock plunging ever deeper and harder into her. Romy tilted her hips up to take him in as far as she could, her eyes on his, tasting blood as he kissed her ferociously.

In these moment, Romy saw nothing else but her love, her Blue. Their connection, forged so quickly all those years ago, had only grown stronger, through the horrific circumstances that nearly killed them both, to the ecstatic joy of Grace's birth. She had never known what it meant to be truly a partnership until Blue, and she thanked the heavens for him every day.

Blue's cock, buried inside her, seemed to grow even larger as she neared her orgasm and they came together, Blue groaning as he shot thick reams of creamy white cum deep into her belly. Romy muffled her cries by biting his shoulder – which only served to make Blue even more aroused and after a few minutes, he was inside her again, almost feral in his desire for her.

. . .

It was almost dawn before they finally feel asleep, having made it to their bedroom at last. Blue wrapped his arms around Romy as they slept, and when they were woken a few hours later by Gracie climbing into their bed, they greeted their daughter happily, listening to her talk excitedly about decorating the tree.

After breakfasting on way too many carbs, they took Grace out into the woods to explore a little. They were surrounded by spruce, and deep fluffy snow, but the sun was out and the air was cold but refreshing.

Later, as Blue gave Grace her lunch, Romy drove down to the little farmer's market in the town at the bottom of the mountain. As well-stocked as their lodge home was, there were still a few pieces that Romy wanted to get by herself – small gifts for Grace's stocking, and some fresh produce.

She browsed the aisles slowly, knowing Grace would have a nap before they decorated the tree anyway, and that Blue had some emails he wanted to catch up on. The farmer's market was full of home-grown produce and freshly butchered meat. Romy bought a large chicken for their Christmas day supper, and grabbed as much fruit as she could handle. She saw some adorable little wooden bears, and was selecting one for Grace when she heard her name.

"Romy? Romy Sasse?"

She turned to see a tall, handsome man with short brown hair and merry hazel eyes twinkling at her. She gaped at him. "Atlas? Atlas Tigri?"

"The very one. How are you, small fry?"

Romy threw her arms around him, hugging him tightly. Atlas Tigri had been one of her best friends from school but she hadn't seen him for years. He had been a quiet, studious type, shy until one got to know him, then he showed his whip-smart intelligence and quick-wit. He had been best friends with her sister Artemis's husband, Dan. Romy studied him now.

"So, Tigri, what gives? I heard you were living in London."

He grinned. "Mostly. But I came home for Christmas this year. Mom is, well, let's say less spry than she used to be, and so I thought I'd lend a hand. My sister's kids are a handful. Luckily Mateo's kid keeps them in line." Atlas, like Romy, was a twin, but unlike Romy, Atlas's twin Mateo was his exact copy – tall, broad and drop dead gorgeous.

"Any kids of your own?"

"Not yet. I hear you're married?"

Romy told him about Blue and Grace. "God, it's good to see you. Why don't you come up to the lodge and have drinks with us? We're here all week."

They swapped cell-phone numbers and Atlas promised to call, kissing her cheek. "So good to see you, small fry."

She was still smiling as she took her groceries to the check-out. The man behind the counter, his lank black hair unshaped and too long, smiled at her. "And how are you this morning?"

Romy gave him a polite smile. "Good, thanks. Just these please."

She was digging around for her wallet when she realized he was staring at her. Uncomfortable, she glanced at the register. "What do I owe you?"

"Seventeen-fifty-three...and maybe your cell-phone number?"

Oh, lord. She tried not to pull a face. "Ah. Sorry." She waved her wedding ring finger. "Very, *very* married."

"Shame."

Annoying creep. "Not for me. Thanks." She went to pick up the brown paper bag, then recoiled, as he placed a very cold, sweaty hand on hers.

"Don't be so hasty. You gave your cell number to that man – why can't I have it?"

Was he for real? Pulling her hand away sharply, Romy glanced around the store and realized they were alone. "Look, you're being completely inappropriate. I don't want to ask for your manager, but I will."

His smile was nasty. "He's out sick today. You're really pretty."

Romy took her bag and headed for the door. In a flash he was in front of her, slamming the door shut and leaning against it. "C'mon now...it's Christmas. Give me some sugar."

Give him some sugar? Romy, despite her unease, had to laugh aloud at that one. "Listen, *boy*," she said, steel in her voice. "Get out of my way right now, and I'll *think* about not reporting you to the police."

He grabbed her shoulders. "I just want to have a little fun. You don't need to be a bitch about it."

What the hell was happening here? Romy calmly put her bag down on the floor then stood to face him. Without warning, she brought her knee up sharply, and smashed it into his groin. The man buckled, cussing her out. Romy calmly picked up her bag of groceries, and walked out of the door, leaving him with a "Go fuck yourself, creep."

It wasn't until she was in the car and driving back up the mountain that she realized she was trembling so violently that she was making the car slide on the icy road. She pulled over and calmed herself down. Closing her eyes, she dragged great lungfuls of air in, feeling her breathing steady, her heart slow. *What the fuck was wrong with the world?*

She heard the whoop of a police car siren as it pulled up behind her and a tall deputy get out. She rolled down the window.

"You okay, ma'am?"

She nodded, then shook her head, the words spilling out, telling him exactly what had happened. His mouth set in a grim line. "Yeah, we've heard rumors. Are you sure you're okay? He didn't hurt you?"

"No, I'm okay, just a little shaken. Why on earth do they employ him?"

The deputy rolled his eyes. "He's the owner's daughter's boyfriend. Look, I'm going to escort you home, Ma'am. If you'd like to make a statement..."

Romy considered. "Actually, I would. There's no reason other women should suffer that creep."

. . .

AT HOME, Blue looked alarmed as she introduced the deputy, Jim, to him and told him what had happened. "That son-of-a-bitch! I'll deal with him." Blue was enraged but both Romy and Jim blocked his way.

"We'll deal with him, sir, don't you worry. Mrs. Allende wants to make a statement and we'll press charges of assault and harassment."

Romy looked slightly guilty. "I'm probably guilty of assault too. I might have kneed him in the balls."

Blue and Jim both grinned. "Did he put his hands on you first, Mrs. Allende?"

Romy nodded and Jim shrugged. "Then it's self-defense. Now, let's take that statement."

AFTER JIM HAD TAKEN her statement and bid them farewell, Blue hugged Romy tightly. "Trouble follows you, *Piccolo*," he said, but laughed, and Romy could see it was mostly from relief.

His use of her nickname reminded her of meeting Atlas. "It went completely out of my mind. I've invited him for drinks one night – I hope you don't mind."

"Not at all, I would like to meet him. It's a pity you didn't walk out of the store with him."

"Ha," Romy said, mildly, "I took care of it."

"Yeah you did, sexy ninja wife." He eyed her appreciatively. "Gracie will be up soon...but I think we could still get one in under the wire."

Romy burst out laughing. "Now, *that's* sexy," she dead-panned, but giggled as Blue swept her into his arms and placed her on the kitchen counter. He pushed her skirt up to her hips, shimmying her panties down her legs, over her boots, which he insisted she kept on. Romy had to admit that they did add to the sensuality of the moment. As Blue thrust his cock into her, she gave a small moan of release, forgetting all her upset, knowing that this man loving her now was all she would ever need.

· · ·

THEY HAD JUST FINISHED DECORATING the tree when the deputy called. "We've arrested him – apparently there are other female customers who have made complaints too. He'll be out on bail soon, I expect, but it's handled."

"Thank you so much," Romy said. "I'm sorry you had to deal with it."

"No problem at all. Been aching to book that creep for years. Merry Christmas, Ma'am."

"And to you, Deputy."

ROMY HUNG UP THE PHONE, gave a thumbs up to a relieved Blue and watched as her daughter was surreptitiously poking at the wrapped gifts under the tree. "I can see you, Gracie Allende."

Gracie gave a chuckle. "Momma, why has Santa brought these ones early?"

"Ah, because you've been a good girl."

"Then I can open them now?" She looked at her parents hopefully.

Romy laughed as Blue picked his daughter up. "Not a chance, monkey. Come on now, Christmas day is only tomorrow, kiddo. Enjoy the anticipation."

"Yes, we're going to watch Christmas movies and eat enough sugar to give us all diabetic comas." Blue said with a grin at his wife, who rolled her eyes.

"Look, Gracie, we're going to make a gingerbread house – want to help?"

ROMY PUT the upsetting incident at the Farmer's market to the back of her mind as she enjoyed the evening with her family. After making a tall but rather crooked gingerbread house, they sat down to watch *Home Alone* and *Home Alone 2* with Gracie – their favorite Christmas movies, before gorging on mac and cheese for their supper.

Despite her assurances that she wouldn't be able to sleep a wink,

Gracie fell asleep in Romy's arms just as the second movie finished and Romy carried her daughter up to bed, tucking her in. She sat on the bed, stroking her daughter's soft face, marveling at the sweet beauty of her. She felt Blue follow her in and they both watched their daughter sleep for a while.

"Isn't she perfect?"

"Just like her mother," Blue said softly and took her hand. He led her quietly out of Gracie's room and to their own bedroom. Inside, he kissed her tenderly, stroking his thumbs over her cheeks, gazing at her with such love-filled eyes, Romy felt weak. "*Ti amo.*" His voice was soft, and sent tingles down her spine.

"*Ti amo*, Blue."

Their love-making this night was slow and leisurely, soaking every moment of sensuality up, enjoying each other's bodies as they moved in perfect rhythm with the other. Romy sighed and shivered through multiple orgasms as Blue made love to her in the indigo moonlight streaming through their window.

Before they fell asleep, Romy and Blue lay talking softly, mostly about their daughter and how excited she would be in the morning.

Blue tucked a lock of hair behind her ear. "I still can't believe we're parents, Romulus."

She grinned at the nickname her family had always given her. "I know, it's just so grown up."

They were quiet for a while, then Romy said "Do you think it's the right time to try for another? Do you even want another?"

Blue grinned. "Baby, I want a *bunch* of kids with you. I was ready for another about three seconds after Gracie was born."

Romy laughed. "Even after I threatened to 'Bobbitt' you if you ever got me knocked up again?"

"Even then. What do you think? I mean, let's be practical, I'd love to carry the kid for you but that ain't gonna happen. So, we're talking about a year of your life, a year out of your career. And with this other thing..."

"Yeah, it'll be complicated. But, I'm thirty-four now. There's a time limit here – okay, so it's not pressing but it's still there. And I want another child, Blue, so badly. I want to give you your son."

Blue kissed her. "I'll be happy as long as they are healthy. I quite like being outnumbered by women."

Romy laughed. "I bet you do. Listen, this isn't the time to make huge decisions like this...let's save that for after tomorrow. But by the end of the week, one way or another, I'm going to have to make some difficult decisions."

"I got your back, beautiful, whatever you decide."

Romy smiled gratefully at him. "As long as I have you and Gracie, I'm good. That's all that matters."

THE NEXT MORNING was a riot of laughter, torn wrapping paper, way too much sugar and one very excited and happy little girl. Romy and Blue played with Gracie, helping her put together her toys, taking her directions (Blue was put on diaper duty for her new doll, Romy sneaked some chocolate spread into the diaper and giggled when she saw his horrified face).

Romy and Blue took turns in playing with Gracie and cooking their celebration meal. Outside, the sun was hidden behind gray clouds heavy with snow, and as evening fell, it began to snow thick flakes and they turned off the lights in the lodge and watched it fall.

A picture-perfect Christmas, Romy thought, and felt a tug in her chest. She didn't want to be away from Blue and Gracie most of her time. And yet her career was so important to her that she couldn't see a way out. She hadn't realized her sadness showed on her face until she and Blue were alone again that night and he asked her what she had been thinking.

"Just about work," she said with a half-smile. "And the thought of leaving you and Gracie in Seattle while I work in Portland...god. No. I can't do it. Especially if we decide to have another baby. I love my job, I *love* it, it's my calling...but I love you and Gracie more. I think I'm going to stay at Rainier Hope. I know it's not the best thing for my career but it is the best thing for me, and our family."

Blue was thoughtful, but he looked unhappy. "I hate that you're having to choose."

"Don't. I got to choose, I wasn't dictated to by you or anyone else. *I* made this decision."

Blue wrapped his arms around her. "I promise, everything I can do that doesn't fall within nepotism or favoring, I will do. I won't let you slip behind your peers."

"You bet your ass I won't," Romy said with a grin. She tangled her fingers in his hair. "I know you'll be the best Chief ever, and I also know you're fair, balanced – with only a hint of bias."

"More than a hint, but thanks." Blue was chuckling.

"Baby...all I really care about is us. I won at life when I met you, when we had Gracie. My Mom is happy, my sisters are doing so great and I get to wake up with you. *God*, I'm a lucky woman."

"Well, shucks." Always unassuming, Blue's face was red, but he grinned anyway. "Then how about we go practice making another baby?"

"I say *yes*," Romy laughed and laughed as he bore her upstairs. "Merry Christmas, baby."

"Merry Christmas, beautiful."

TWO DAYS LATER, her decision made, Romy felt a weight fall from her shoulders. She called the hospital in Portland and expressed her regrets but turned the job down. They were disappointed but offered her any position she wanted should she change her mind. Romy watched Blue and Gracie playing and knew she had made the absolute right decision for her.

ROMY OPENED the door and greeted Atlas as he trudged through the snow. "Hey, small fry," he said with a grin as she hugged him.

"Come and meet Blue and Gracie."

A half hour later, and Atlas, with his natural charm, had won over both Romy's husband and daughter. Gracie climbed onto Atlas's knee and told him all about her Christmas presents and Atlas chatted easily with her. He and Blue found common ground easily, both men's sense of humor jelling almost straight away.

Later, the adults shared a late supper. Blue opened some champagne. "To old – and new – friends," he grinned and they tapped their flutes.

"Well, I do have some news. I didn't mention it the other day because it was still being worked out but...I'm relocating back to Seattle permanently." Atlas grinned at Romy's surprise.

"That's wonderful...but what about your business in London?"

"My partner has just bought me out. He knew my heart didn't lie in it anymore, selling pharmaceuticals. More and more I felt like I was taking from the world rather than giving back."

Romy nodded. "Fair enough, but what will you do now?"

"I'm glad you asked because I might need some advice." Atlas pulled out a crumpled piece of paper. "A couple of years ago, one of my nieces was assaulted. She was at college, alone in a study room, and her boyfriend, who she'd just broken up with, found her and... You can guess. Since then, it's been bugging me that there isn't a safe house in the city that also helps those battered women – and to a lesser extent, men, who can't afford medical expenses. So, me, and a couple of other local entrepreneurs are doing just that. Seattle's first secure hostel with a full medical staff. I also want to make sure that we have a fully operational surgical facility – and an emergency room. Basically, somewhere to go when things are desperate. Eventually, I'd like to extend it to the homeless too."

Romy and Blue looked at each other in amazement. "But that's fantastic," Romy said, shaking her head in amazement. "God, Atlas... if I had had that when I left Dacre..." There was a lump in her throat. "Atlas..."

Blue rubbed her back, seeing she was close to tears. "And you need us to headhunt medical and surgical staff?"

Atlas nodded. "Please...obviously, this is a voluntary role, so asking docs to give up their time and pay-packet to do so might be difficult and there'll be no recriminations if candidates decide they can't make it work. I do need a chief of surgery though."

"I'll do it."

Both Blue and Atlas looked at Romy. She returned their gazes steadily. "It's perfect. Look, Atlas, these past few days we've been going around and around trying to find a role for me which doesn't smack of nepotism but also won't tamp down my career. This is it. Don't you think, Blue?"

Blue nodded slowly, and Romy could see him working things out in his head. "Yeah...yes, I think it is perfect. What do you think, Atlas?"

Atlas looked a little shell-shocked. "Well, I mean...god, really? You would do this? Train my staff? Be our head of surgery? For free?"

Romy started to laugh. "Are you kidding me? *Of course*. There is just one thing. There's a good chance I might be pregnant again soon, so we'd have to work around that."

Atlas held his hands up. "Girl, even an hour of your time would mean the world to us – I think we can accommodate a pregnancy." He laughed. "But we should slow down, discuss this more fully when we're not hopped up on your good champagne."

But Romy could see how excited he was and later, after Atlas had gone home, she smiled at Blue. "This is it, isn't it? This is what I *should* be doing. Everything has been pointing towards this."

Blue studied her. "You know what, Romulus Sasse? You are my freaking heroine; do you know that? My absolute superstar Wonder Woman. Yes, baby, I agree. Everything's has been leading to this. It's not only a way to give back, but to finally get the stain of Dacre from your memories."

"Exactly. Honestly, baby," Romy wrapped her arms around her husband's neck, "I can't wait to get started."

"Let's go celebrate."

"Take me to bed, Allende."

THREE MONTHS LATER, Atlas's clinic opened its doors.

. . .

Six months after that, Zachery Stuart Allende was born, with his twin sister Rosa following six minutes later. Their mother and father looked down at their newborn twins and knew their family was now complete.

The End.

Created with Vellum